The Stockton Saga 3

The Stockton Saga 3

A Man to Reckon With

Steven Douglas Glover

iUniverse LLC
Bloomington

The Stockton Saga 3
A Man to Reckon With

iUniverse books may be ordered through booksellers or by contacting:

iUniverse LLC
1663 Liberty Drive
Bloomington, IN 47403
www.iuniverse.com
1-800-Authors (1-800-288-4677)

ISBN: 978-1-4917-0226-0 (sc)
ISBN: 978-1-4917-0227-7 (ebk)

Printed in the United States of America

iUniverse rev. date: 08/06/2013

CONTENTS

Preface

The Stockton Saga began as a short story for a friend. The response in her words was, "Put all of your Cole Stockton stories together and you will have a great novel." Other friends and acquaintances read my accounts of the old west with enthusiasm, asking me to add to the narratives. This positive feedback inspired me to continue relating the tales of adventure and moral consequence of a Deputy United States Marshal that have flooded my mind for years.

Thus, the series began with book one, *Stockton Saga: Dawn of the Gunfighter*, relating the heritage, birth and character development of Cole Stockton. *The Stockton Saga 2: Star of Justice*, recounts his early years as a lawman as well as his chance meeting and enduring relationship with Laura Sumner.

Each new character, event, and locale penned calls me to place my central character, Cole Stockton, in yet other situations that bring justice to the frontier of the late 19th Century. Each saga introduces and further develops his charter as well as the characters of those unique individuals who share the frontier with Cole.

This book, *The Stockton Saga 3: A Man to Reckon With* resumes where *Star of Justice* left Cole, and continues his life of danger, intrigue and fulfillment as a Deputy U.S. Marshal in the Colorado Territory.

Immeasurable appreciation goes to long-time friend, Monti Lynn Eastin, for the portrayal and psyche of the character Laura Sumner. Her support of me expanding the short stories, and continually encouraging me to publish them, is warmly appreciated.

My immense gratitude goes to Gay Lynn Auld whose time and effort reviewing and editing this manuscript provided invaluable assistance. Her advice for expansion and rewrite were paramount to the production of this book.

Singular thanks to Linda Glover, without whose review and support this book would not have been published.

Very special thanks to the steadfast fans who continue to read my stories, provide feedback and call for more.

Steven Douglas Glover
Round Rock, Texas
July 23, 2013

Unfortunately, 2012 was a year of loss for me. I humbly dedicate this novel to the memory of three of my most avid fans and to the memory of the western author that inspired me to write my own stories.

First and foremost, I dedicate this book to the memory of my mother.

Verna Ellen Krenke Glover
Dec 21, 1923-June 21, 2012

Secondly, I dedicate this book to the memory of my sister-in-law

Vesta Carol Hillsamer Williams
May 31, 1931-June 6, 2012

Thirdly, I dedicate this book to the memory of a most beautiful 101 year old lady who read my stories and consistently asked for more.

Jane Angstadt Day
Oct 2, 1911-October 11, 2012

And to the memory of

Louis L'Amour
1908-1988

Chapter One

The Black Stallion

The early dawn filtered sunlight slowly over the mountain tops to light the Southern Colorado valleys and slopes where wild horse herds roamed in search of fair grazing. One herd in particular, led by a magnificent coal-black stallion, had been the target of many a horse trapper, to no good luck.

No one had been able to track or capture this herd. Their leader was as smart as they come.

This particular morning found the stallion standing on high ground, above his herd of fillies, colts, and spring-born foals. His head raised high in the morning breeze, nostrils flaring, to catch various scents riding on the soft breeze. He turned continuously to watch every movement, however so slight.

Suddenly, nervousness touched the stallion's being, without any apparent reason. He stood ever so still, ears pricked and straining for any sound that would signal danger for the herd. Any such sound or quick movement would cause him to bolt his herd of twenty-five or so wild stock into a fast run for freedom.

Momentarily, it came—a slight creak of leather, followed by the distant whinny of another horse. A few horsemen burst out of a ravine to the left, lariats cradled at the ready. Other riders bolted out of the pines along the tree line to the fore of the herd. The wild horse hunters drove at the herd with wild yells and swinging lassos.

The sleek black rose up on hind legs, forelegs pawing the air. He screamed the alarm, and then galloped into the center of his herd, pushing them toward an escape route. The riders gained on the herd.

Then, the wranglers rode wildly along both sides of the herd, containing them, driving them to exhaustion. Mares and foals slowed, unable to keep the pace of escape and evasion.

The stallion raced to the forefront of his herd, leading them in a wild dash to remain free. A trio of well-mounted horse hunters closed in on the front-runners, centering on the black.

The stallion's senses sharpened and he knew he had to run for his life. Hooves dug into the turf as he stretched out into a full run. His dark mane and tail flew like banners in the wind; powerful muscles rippled as the ground fell away under his hooves.

Within moments, the riders trailed far behind the black. He was making good on his reputation as the most elusive animal in the wilds of Colorado. The tiring stallion suddenly swerved into a stand of aspen and onto an old trail known only to a few old trappers and the inhabitants of the wilds.

Suddenly, there was a quick movement to the right. The noose of a lariat sailed through the air, landing directly around the stallion's neck, slipping closed.

The rider, highly experienced at this work, quickly tied off the other end of the rope to the saddle horn, and the black stallion jerked back, the noose tightening around his long, sleek neck.

"Brace yourself, Mickey! Hold him!" commanded the rider and the stout mustang responded gamely.

The stallion reared and bucked against the rope, ever trying to free himself, but the capturing mount, well trained, moved quickly to counter his every move. Intense minutes slowly ticked by as the evasive stallion employed every means known to man to escape the unfamiliar rope around his neck.

The rope held, and after a slow half-hour of futile effort, the powerful stallion settled down and stood looking at his captor.

The rider, a dark haired young woman dressed in Levi's, leather chaps, wide-brimmed black hat, and sweat-stained dark blue shirt, sat quietly in the saddle looking over the *prize*.

She spoke with soft reassuring tones while carefully drawing the rope to a shorter length. The stallion moved slowly toward her, as she continued to speak softly to the magnificent horse. Finally, the black stallion stood beside her and her mount, a slightly smaller but strongly-built black horse.

Laura Sumner spoke to her mount. "Alright, Mickey, you did good. Let's take our new friend home." Laura touched heel to Mickey and they headed back toward the main herd. The herd nervously milled around, having been captured in its entirety by the other riders.

Laura Sumner's riders grinned with delight when they saw her coming up the embankment with the stallion in tow. She returned their smiles as her foreman, Judd Ellison spoke, "By God, Laura, you got him. You're going to be the envy of all the neighboring ranchers—and a few more."

Laura led the black stallion with Mickey in the lead. The remaining stock of the wild herd followed the stallion back to Laura's ranch with no further incident. Laura's wranglers herded the group into the large holding corral beside the stables, while she led the stallion to a separate, but well-constructed, corral at the other side of the stable.

The black was a special catch, and would be treated as such. Laura led into the corral, closed in on the stallion, and removed the rope from around his neck. The stallion moved away from her to run around and around the corral.

Laura moved to the gate. Judd momentarily opened it for her and Mickey to exit, then quickly closed it and the cross bar slid into place.

Laura dismounted and climbed the corral bars. She took a long deep breath and exhaled fully, the first since she had caught the stallion. Her crystal blue eyes were bright with excitement at having been the one to finally outsmart and catch the elusive horse. Her thoughts turned to how she would proceed with training this catch. She smiled knowingly to herself.

She could hardly contain herself, thinking about how Cole Stockton would take the news. He would be justly proud of her accomplishment. He had complimented her horsemanship before, and now, he would see her sitting atop this magnificent stallion.

Laura closed her eyes for a second and could just see Cole's face—that silly grin, his eyes shining with distinct pleasure. Yes, he would be proud of her. Cole Stockton was due back from his latest trip to the Territorial Court in a few days, and she planned to have made great progress with this horse by then. This stallion would be the newest in her personal string of mounts.

The rest of the horse herd would be sorted out and broken to saddle; the choice stock kept for breeding. Laura would find a market for the remaining animals. She considered the army and miners to be good potential buyers.

Laura expected a good return for the work that her wranglers had put into this roundup and drive. They had almost three hundred head of saddle broken stock, and now was the time to sell them.

Miners needed both good mounts and working horses. They had planned to start a drive to the mining camps within a week, and she was anxiously waiting for this trip. It would be exciting. But, for now, Laura pondered her prize stallion. She would begin his training early the very next morning.

* * *

Early morning found Laura Sumner decked out in her horse busting outfit of Levi's, boots, spurs, leather chaps, blue denim shirt, and rumpled black "lucky" Stetson. Her long dark hair was tied in a ponytail.

She stood at the special corral drinking a cup of hot coffee, watching the black stallion prance nervously around the enclosure. She marveled at the power in the black's muscles.

Three of Laura's ranch hands ambled over to stand silently next to her. All three knew what she was thinking—they, also, were dressed in their bronc riding gear. In short order, they would be working the main group of newly acquired horses.

Two more wranglers joined the group. They would be watching out for Laura, just in case she needed assistance with the black stallion.

"Well, boys," she said with a deep breath followed by a long exhale, and taking a coiled lariat in hand, "let's get it done."

Laura opened the gate to the special corral, quickly stepped inside, then closed the gate behind her. The black stopped prancing and stood looking at her, while pawing the ground. "Good morning, boy," she softly said—still standing stationary. The black's ears pricked up.

Laura took a step toward the stallion. The black moved away from her, then whirled suddenly and came charging toward her. She moved swiftly out of the way, shaking out a loop as she did so.

She quickly moved to the center of the corral, swinging the lariat and widening the loop. The black ran around the corral dodging the swinging rope. He swirled to and fro, but Laura stayed with him, countering his every move until finally, the loop sailed into the air and encircled the black's neck.

Laura settled the loop, then tightened it, racing to the hitching post in the center of the arena. She looped it around the post, and ducked just in time to avoid being run down by the black and tied up in her own rope.

She pulled hard on the free line, and it quickly shortened the play. The black turned and fought the line. Laura walked away back to the gate and stood there watching the black's movements.

The stallion continued to fight the rope for another fifteen minutes. The rope held and finally, he settled down.

Laura walked back out into the corral with the two wranglers. One held a blindfold, hackamore bridle, saddle blanket, and saddle.

Laura continually spoke softly to the stallion—calming him somewhat.

Finally, they got the blind on him, and he stood quietly while Laura slipped on the hackamore. She placed the saddle blanket on his back, and he flinched a bit. She then positioned the saddle on him. The unknown weight bothered him. Laura felt shivers surge through the horse as she tightened the cinches.

"O.K., boys, let's let him ponder that gear for a bit. We'll have another cup of coffee."

Laura slipped the blind from the horse, and rejoined the two ranch hands. They walked off, leaving the black to buck and shake in futile effort to rid himself of the foreign objects on his back.

Laura and the two wranglers stood at the corral bars watching the movements of the horse. Periodically, when Laura spoke soothingly to the stallion, his ears would prick up—he seemed to like the sound of her voice.

An hour or so later, Laura stepped back into the corral, the blindfold in her back pocket. Once again she slowly moved toward the animal, calling to him softly. The animal watched her approach, unsure of his next move.

Laura got close enough to stroke the animal's neck, then slowly and purposely took out the blindfold.

Long minutes later, the horse's eyes were covered. Laura continued speaking gently to the animal. The other two wranglers entered the corral and stood with her.

The rope was removed from the animal's neck. Laura put boot to the stirrup, and swung quickly into the saddle, squirming for the best position. She grabbed the reins of the hackamore securely in her hand, took a long, deep breath, and nodded to the wranglers.

One wrangler pulled the slip knot on the blind, and quickly moved out of the way.

The stallion stood still for only a moment, then—all the pent up fury of captivity uncoiled like a giant spring. Laura felt the sudden tightening of the stallion's muscles and set her jaw.

The stallion unwound like a sprung steel trap, and she was suddenly riding high in the air, teeth rattling, and jolting back to the ground, back up into the air again. From that point, it was *who flung the chunk* all over the corral.

The wranglers cheered Laura on with shouts of "Ride him, Laura! Show that stallion who's boss around here."

In a contest of animal spirit against horsemanship, each felt determined to beat the other at this game of wit and endurance.

The stallion won the first round when he suddenly tucked his long neck between his legs, while his hindquarters went high into the air. Laura lost her grip on the horse and went flying to land on her bottom, facing away from the horse, and spitting out dirt and dust.

Laura's wranglers both winced, but looked away valiantly, as Laura slowly got to her feet rubbing her sore behind. She turned quickly to face the stallion who stood there looking at her, as if to say—"Hey, this is fun, let's do it again." He was mocking her.

Laura took another deep breath, spoke to the horse, and made her way to his side.

Surprisingly, the stallion stood still for her to mount. However, just as soon as he felt her weight in the saddle, the second round of *who's the boss* started.

The stallion reared, bucked, sun-fished, swirled, and tried to shake the living daylights out of the rider who stuck to that saddle like she belonged there. The stallion stopped dead still for a moment, only to gather a second wind, before the fury began again. Laura held on for dear life as the bucking intensified.

Seconds later, Laura once again sailed from the saddle to land hard on the ground. She was a bit longer getting up this time. Her entire body ached from the repeated physical pounding, but she was still game.

Laura walked the animal down, took up the reins, and pulled herself into the saddle. Once more the untamed horse reared and bucked continuously, leaving Laura exhausted. Her arms were heavy, making it difficult to hold on. Yet, she was determined to see this round through.

Minutes passed slowly in the wild whirlwind of horseflesh and rider. Dust filled the air as the stallion bucked in circles, then swirled to buck in the opposite direction. Laura's Stetson flew off as she felt herself lose her grip again.

Once again on the hard ground of the corral, the young horsewoman lay gasping for her breath to return. Foolishly, she attempted to stand quickly, lost her balance and crumbled back to the ground. Her two wranglers quickly entered the corral to help Laura to her feet.

Laura shook her head as she mumbled hoarsely, "This is the toughest horse I've ever tried to ride. I've got to rest and think this one out. See me to the house, boys. We'll continue this tomorrow morning."

The wranglers helped Laura to the ranch house, then returned to the corral to catch up with the black stallion and unsaddle him. Once free of the trappings, the animal circled the corral in the manner of a victory run.

* * *

Once in her room, Laura collapsed on the bed. She was sore head to toes. Momentarily, the young woman was liberal with muscle soothing liniment. Every muscle was on fire. As her body calmed, she thought about the black stallion. She began to question her ability as a horsewoman.

After sundown, Laura emerged from the house dressed in a robe. She lingered on the porch to take in the coolness of the night air, closing her eyes to take in the unmistakable fragrance of wild flowers that calmed her senses.

A smile came to Laura's face as she suddenly realized what she must do. She stepped off the porch, moving toward the stables where she approached the black stallion. The animal stood watching the woman. At the stall entrance, she spoke in soft tones to the magnificent creature.

To her amazement, the horse moved toward her. Laura stroked the black's head and neck as she continued soft words of comfort. "You are such a wonderful horse, but today was no way to treat a lady. We need to do better. Tomorrow, we will come to an understanding."

Laura returned to her home a short time later. She smiled as she lay down, only to sit up quickly massaging her back. She called out to herself, "Ouch! I'm still sore. I hope that I don't show it in the morning. I have got to be more determined. I want that stallion for my second personal mount."

With pillows cradling her back, and a dream of riding the black stallion, Laura slipped into an easy slumber.

*   *   *

Early the next morning, Laura Sumner stepped out onto the porch clad once again in her horse-taming outfit. The aroma of liniment filled the air as she muttered to herself, "O.K., Boss Lady, today is the day that the black and I become one. I've got it to do!"

Laura stepped off the porch to walk to the corral where her foreman, Judd Ellison, had the black stallion saddled and ready for the challenge. Judd greeted Laura with a smile and "Good morning, Miss Laura."

Laura returned the smile. "Good morning, Judd. Thank you for getting him ready for our workout. Well, let's not waste any time. I'd like you to watch out for me." With those words, Laura entered the corral and walked toward the black. She spoke soothingly to the animal as she gathered up the reins. A moment later, she put boot to stirrup and rose into the saddle.

Immediately, the black took off in a run around the corral, then moved into a series of cyclone twists and bucks. Laura stuck with him, her muscles aching and bones jarring each time the stallion hit the ground.

All at once, Laura began yelling to the animal in spurts of breathless dialog, "Come on, you magnificent horse! Show me what you got! That's not good enough! Ugh! That was pitiful! Yah! Come on! Give me your best! Is that all you've got? Let's do it! Buck harder! Yah, that's more like it!"

Wranglers from all corners of the ranch yard heard the commotion and ran to the corral to watch Laura fight the wild out of the most spirited animal they had ever seen. The men crowded the corral bars to watch this contest between pure wild and Boss Wrangler. Minutes passed quickly as the ranch hands each held their breath. Laura had not once been thrown off the horse.

With this new day and new battle, there was a different aura in the air. The black was tiring. Laura was *riding high* as the stallion repeated all the moves of the previous day, however the lady stayed with him, countering his every move.

Finally, after a long hour, the black trotted around the corral, guided by the soft spoken woman known as Laura Sumner. When she dismounted, the black followed her, recognizing Laura had won. When cheers went up from the wrangler crowd, Laura smiled for a moment before breaking into teary laughter as she stroked the neck of her newest mount.

Chapter Two

Pandemonium in Court

A muffled din filled the Colorado Territorial courtroom as the twelve-man jury returned to the room. Once they were seated in the jury box, Judge Joshua Bernard Wilkerson turned to the jury foreman. "Has the jury reached a verdict in the case of the Territory of Colorado versus Devin Williams?"

The tall, well dressed man selected foreman of the jury by his peers stood erect and nodded affirmatively while unfolding a sheet of paper. "Yes, Your Honor, the jury has reached a verdict." He paused a long moment to clear his throat, "We the jury find Devin Williams guilty of murder as charged."

Devin Williams, a powerfully built man, suddenly bolted from his seat beside his court appointed attorney. "The hell you say!" He raised his right hand to point at the jury as he bellowed out, "You'll all be sorry for this day! You'll all pay for this, I swear it!"

Williams then turned and grabbed his lawyer, Theodore James, by the throat as he seemed to strangle the life out of the man. He shouted as he choked Mr. James, "Here's your payment for services!" Women in the gallery delivered shrieks of fear. "Oh my God!" screamed one woman, "He's killing the poor man."

Deputy Marshals Quinn and Bradley rushed to Williams attempting to force release of his hold on Mr. James, but Williams tightened his grip with one hand while he slugged Marshal Bradley hard in the face with the other. Bradley staggered backward with the impact, colliding with Marshal Quinn before falling to the floor out cold. Quinn stumbled, reaching out to grab Williams for an instant as he too slipped to the floor, struggling to regain his composure. Lawyer James gasped for breath as he thrashed wildly about in vain attempt to release himself from the big man's death grip.

At the first violent outburst, Deputy U.S. Marshal Cole Stockton bolted from the spectator gallery and just as quickly into the fray. His hand reached behind his back with lightning speed to produce a Colt revolver. He spoke loudly as he forcefully laid the barrel of the revolver along the side of the violent man's head, "That's enough of that!"

Williams reeled from the strike to his head, pulling James to the floor along with him, then slowly released his hold. Lawyer James panted for breath as he fought to claw himself from underneath Williams. Spectators rose from their seats to gain a better view of the melee. Pandemonium reined in the courtroom.

"Order in the Court! Order in the Court!" commanded Judge Wilkerson as he struck the gavel down, again and again. "Bailiff! Send for Doc Taylor immediately and then bring that man Williams before the bench."

John Taney, the bailiff, and Deputy Marshal Nate Quinn reached down to drag Williams to his feet. Handcuffs were quickly produced and locked around Williams' wrists at his backside. The prisoner shook his head from side to side attempting to clear his mind from the momentary daze resulting from Stockton's blow. Blood trickled down the right side of his head. He was only slightly cognizant as the two law officers held him up in front of the bench to learn his fate.

"Devin Williams," Judge Wilkerson announced in solemn voice, "your sentencing will take place at one o'clock tomorrow afternoon, after a doctor has examined you to deem that you are able to comprehend my words. Deputies, escort Mr. Williams back to his cell for safe keeping. Did someone go for the doctor?" Bailiff Taney acknowledged that a runner was on his way for the doctor.

The judge waited until the prisoner was ushered from the courtroom, then turned his attention to Cole Stockton. "Marshal Stockton, as I understand it, you are not in this courtroom as a guard but rather as a witness. Am I correct on that point?"

Stockton knew what was coming as he grinned back at Judge Wilkerson, "Yes, Your Honor, I am merely here as a witness in the case at hand, as well as a spectator."

Judge Wilkerson appeared stern as he cleared his throat and announced in an authoritative voice, "Mr. Stockton, witnesses must be unarmed in my courtroom. For your obvious neglect of my rules,

I hereby fine you five dollars for carrying a concealed weapon in my court."

The judge then reached under his robe and produced a roll of bills from which he withdrew a five-dollar note. He then extended his hand toward Henry, the Court Clerk. Henry took the money as Wilkerson announced, "The fine is paid, Mr. Stockton. In the future, please see that you adhere to the rules of the court." The judge then struck his gavel and announced for all to hear, "Court is now adjourned until one o'clock tomorrow. Marshal Stockton, please meet with me in my chambers after lunch."

Cole Stockton cocked his head to one side and raised his eyebrows inquiringly as the judge grinned at him a moment before he turned to leave the bench to his private chambers. John Taney stood and called out, "All rise!" The judge disappeared from the courtroom.

Spectators gathered around Stockton, patting him on the back. Several men pumped his hand while giving thanks for a job well done to eliminate mayhem in the courtroom.

Cole thought, "Now what? What could he possibly want of me now? Well, guess I'll get a bite to eat. I'll find out soon enough. I sure hope he doesn't have another time-consuming task in mind. I promised Laura that I'd be there to ride along on her next drive to sell her horses."

Chapter Three

A Special Prisoner

I left the courthouse and ambled over to where I call home when at the Colorado Territorial Seat: Ma Sterling's boarding house. As I walked, I thought through the court proceedings in the Williams case.

As the arresting officer, I'd been summoned to testify against Devin Williams in a triple murder case. I had investigated the circumstances and then testified that Williams had tracked three prospectors within the wilds of the Colorado Territory.

Sneaking up on them in the middle of the night, he had savagely slit their throats while they slept and rummaged their pokes. Finding nothing, he had sacked their belongings, taking pocket watches and rings.

The monster had even pried three gold teeth with his belt knife from one of the hapless men. He left with their pack animals, supplies, and assorted goods. The murderer had traded or sold them to persons of questionable repute as he traveled throughout the area.

Having been on his trail for two weeks, I finally had caught up with Williams at a trading post where he was devouring food and slopping whiskey copiously. He was as belligerent then, as he had become in the courtroom. Only the quick threat of my blowing his brains out had settled him down to be taken in cuffs back to Denver and the territorial jail. Upon searching his person for hidden weapons, I had discovered the damning evidence of a gold pocket watch known to belong to one of the murdered miners. I had testified as such. My testimony seemed to be the words that sealed his conviction. In my mind's eye, I saw justice sealing the fate of Devin Williams.

Momentarily, I walked into Ma Sterling's parlor and caught the enticing aroma of an apple pie in the oven. When I entered the dining room, other guests were enjoying bowls of homemade vegetable soup with fresh bread and thick slices of cheese.

I hung my Stetson on the back of a chair as another of the boarders, James Wooten, passed the soup tureen my way. Nodding my thanks, I ladled the soup into a bowl at my place. Wooten looked at me with questioning eyes. "How did the trial go, Marshal Stockton?"

"The jury found Williams guilty," was all I said as I turned to partake of my soup.

There were still a few boarders chatting when I glanced at the wall clock and decided it was time to meet with Judge Wilkerson to learn what devilish task he had in store for me this time.

Fifteen minutes later found me standing in Clerk Henry's office while he went in to tell the Judge Wilkerson that I was present to see him. It didn't take but a few moments before Henry returned, and holding the door to the judge's chambers open, bid me enter.

Judge Wilkerson sat behind his large wooden desk pondering the telegram he held as I entered and stood stone still in front of him. I recalled the years of our association. He was a man of his word. I felt proud to serve him and call him a friend.

The judge suddenly looked up at me over his wire-rimmed spectacles and that sly smile that always signaled that I was about to be put to the task spread across his face. "Sit down, Cole", he said, indicating a chair in front of his desk.

I looked into his deep gray eyes for only a second, then just blurted it out, "Tell me it ain't so, Judge."

"Why, whatever do you mean, Cole?" he grinned back at me.

"Well, Judge, I've known you for quite a while, and whenever you get that cat-that-swallowed-the-canary look on your face, it usually means that you've got some kind of special task that is going to fry my bacon."

Judge Wilkerson leaned forward across his desk, nodding affirmatively. His expression turned serious as he pondered his next statement. "Cole, I've just this morning received a telegram advising me of a special prisoner being held at a place called Fletcher's Station. That's a Northwest Mounted Police post about ten miles into Saskatchewan Province, Canada. It seems that they have apprehended a fugitive whom I issued a murder warrant for and they've agreed to hold this person to extradite back to us."

He took a deep breath before continuing, "I want you to go there and escort the fugitive back to face my court. You will take the train from Denver to the Wyoming Territory, Cheyenne to be exact. Once there, check in at Fort D.A. Russell. You are authorized to be outfitted with an extra mount for your prisoner as well as a pack horse and provisions for the remainder of your journey to Canada, which will have to be by horseback."

I started to protest and the judge saw it in my eyes immediately. "Don't bother to protest," he countered. "It's settled. I've chosen you for this task because you are one of my most trusted deputies and I know that you will succeed. Out of my office now. Go pack for the journey. Be in my office at eight o'clock sharp in the morning and I'll have rail tickets for you and your horse as well as the necessary documents to acquire custody of this special prisoner."

I emitted a long sigh. It would be at least three, if not four weeks, before I could return to Laura's ranch at Miller's Station. I would send a telegram advising her. It appeared quite likely that Laura would start her horse drive without my assistance. The thought hit me then that there was a chance that I just might meet up with her horse herd on the way back through Wyoming. If not, then I would follow their trail to ride back with them when I was finished with the duty at hand. I sure hated to disappoint her, but sworn duty comes first.

Leaving the courthouse, I stopped in at the rail depot to send Laura my telegram. Afterward, I walked back to Ma Sterling's to ready my duffle for the trip. I couldn't help but wonder, what was it about this special prisoner that had Judge Wilkerson so deeply concerned. Well, it wasn't for me to question; it was only for me to carry out the judge's wishes.

* * *

The next morning, following a hot breakfast of eggs, bacon, a short stack of flapjacks sweetened with molasses and a steaming cup of black coffee, I saddled up Chino, my big roan, and tied my duffle behind the saddle. Chino looked at me so as to say, "Looks like we are going a-traveling. Great! Let's get started." He was mighty frisky as we stepped out into the dirt street and trotted to the courthouse.

Leaving Chino at the hitching rack, I went upstairs to enter Henry's office. He ushered me directly into the judge's chambers. He was just signing the extradite document allowing me to take charge of one person named *Charley Westbrook*. He put the document into an envelope, then handed it to me along with rail tickets for me and Chino to Cheyenne, Wyoming. There were also return train tickets for Chino and me as well as the prisoner.

"Marshal Stockton," the judge said, "this is a very important mission that you are on. Take care in your travel for there may be peril along the way. I trust that you will handle any such circumstance with utmost prudence. Good luck to you."

I took the document and tickets from the judge and put them into the inside pocket of my jacket prior to leaving the judge's office. I wondered then just what the judge knew about peril along the way. Prudence? That word seemed out of ordinary for the judge, but I figured that he meant to be ready for whatever came my way.

I climbed into the saddle and Chino trotted to the rail depot where the train to Cheyenne was being readied. I showed my tickets to the station clerk. He pointed to the stock car where a few men were leading other mounts and unsaddled horses into the car. I led Chino inside, positioning him for a rocking, jolting ride. He seemed happy to have company in the car with him. Next, I found myself a seat in the passenger car close to the rear entrance as other passengers boarded the car. Out of habit I looked them over carefully. There were a couple of cattlemen, some couples, a family of four, a few ranch hands, and a couple of young ladies accompanied by a matronly woman whom I took as their trusted custodian for the trip. The women took seats across the aisle from me.

With about a hundred miles to Cheyenne and this train traveling at the unheard of speed of about twenty miles an hour, it would be about a five hour trip. I had a full seat to myself. I figured to take a nap while the train rocked and swayed its way to our destination and readied my Stetson to cover my eyes once the train got going.

Suddenly, the whistle blew and the bell clanged. The conductor yelled "All aboard!" and the gigantic engine churned wheels as it chugged into movement. The car lurched forward, causing the ladies to grab onto armrests to steady themselves. It took only a few minutes for them to lose themselves in chatter about their upcoming shopping trip in the great city of Cheyenne.

* * *

The train slid to a grinding halt at the depot with bell ringing, whistle blowing, and passengers holding on tight to avoid being tossed into one another. Once to a full stop, the conductor strolled through the car announcing "Cheyenne, Wyoming Territory. Please watch your step as you disembark. Gentlemen, please assist the ladies as they take to the platform."

Gents quickly helped the young ladies down the steps of the car. I found myself reaching up to take the hand of a matronly woman as she held her skirts up slightly to watch where she was stepping. I felt appreciated with her quick smile and "Thank you, Sir." I watched for a minute or so while the ladies made their way along the wooden platform to enter the depot. Seeing them dressed up in their fine dresses reminded me a bit of Laura dressed up for the spring dance at Miller's Station. That thought made me smile a bit.

Then, I made my way alongside the train to the stock car where a few men had assembled, waiting on the workers to open the car door and set the stock unloading platform steadfast so we could retrieve our animals. We entered the car amid horses stamping about, anxious to disembark. Chino was glad to see me. I led him into the fresh air, sunshine, and a watering trough. After he had a good drink, I climbed into the saddle.

Turning to one of the rail workers, I inquired, "Which way to Fort Russell?" He pointed northwest. Chino and I got a good look at the city of Cheyenne as we headed toward the fort.

Cheyenne had become a booming city of probably three hundred businesses. There were saloons a plenty, a stock yard, drug store, barber shop, mercantile stores galore, millinery, lawyers, a post office, stagecoach depot, warehouses, churches, and a school.

Before long, Chino and I found ourselves at the entrance to Fort D.A. Russell. There was no stockade. Rather, an open quadrangle of buildings formed on the prairie along Crow Creek. I made my way to the post headquarters and requested to speak to the post adjutant. Within minutes, I was ushered in to meet with Captain Jim Lloyd who advised me that His Honor Judge Wilkerson had provided the commanding officer with a telegram outlining my mission and requesting his support.

Captain Lloyd looked at me questioningly, "Marshal Stockton, would you be ready to travel at sunup tomorrow morning? We have a cavalry patrol departing then for points north. In fact, they're traveling to the Montana Territory."

I answered him, "Yes, Captain, I'll be ready. I'd enjoy some company on this trip."

"Fine," replied Captain Lloyd. "I'll ensure that Sergeant Otis Hoffmeister knows that you will accompany them to Montana. From that point, Marshal, you are on your own. I don't think that I need to tell you that it is no picnic on that route. That territory is wild beyond all imagination, filled with hills, deep ravines that the Sioux call *coulees* and," he paused a moment reflectively, "we suspect, hostiles like Sitting Bull and his people. Take care, Marshal Stockton, keep a keen eye out on your journey."

Captain Lloyd paused a moment, "And one more thing, Marshal Stockton. Please join me and the other bachelor officers for dinner in the officer's mess at six o'clock." I voiced my appreciation for the supper invitation and took my leave of the captain.

Next, I went to the quartermaster building where the corporal there outfitted a pack for me with various supplies. He included coffee, salt pork, beans, oats, and a few potatoes. He advised that he would have the pack animal outfitted and ready for me at daybreak. I thanked the corporal and took Chino to the cavalry stables for the night.

After unsaddling the roan, I stood rubbing him down when a rather large man wearing sergeant chevrons approached me. In a German accent yet in quite good English, the man spoke, "Marshal Stockton, I am Sergeant Hoffmeister. We will be riding together for a while. If there is anything that you need, please let me know." I thanked the sergeant as he clicked his heels together, throwing me a snappy salute before turning to go about his duties.

After seeing to Chino, I took my duffle, saddlebags, and Winchester rifle in hand and walked over to the room I had been afforded for the night. Promptly at five o'clock, retreat sounded and the post flag was lowered. I stood on the porch of my temporary quarters to watch the ceremony with interest. Afterward, a bugle call announced supper time and the troopers not assigned to guard duty made their way to a mess hall to partake of the evening meal. I joined Captain Lloyd and five other junior officers in the officer's mess where we enjoyed antelope steak, baked potatoes, and boiled carrots. Coffee was plentiful, rich and dark.

The conversation at supper was congenial, the officers taking care not to question my mission. Afterward, we enjoyed a smoke on the porch while listening to a few troopers playing guitars and singing softly. There must've been an Irishman or two in the group because I recognized the haunting strains of *The Last Rose of Summer* which caused me to reflect on Laura and our relationship. At that moment, I longed to see her face and gaze into those crystal blue eyes. I retired for the evening with her in the recesses of my mind, bringing a smile to my face.

I arose the next morning when bugles sounded reveille. I dressed and made my way to the officer's mess for a quick breakfast after which I made my way to the stables and found Sergeant Hoffmeister and ten troopers saddling up and forming for travel. My pack animal was already outfitted and waiting alongside the patrol's packhorse. Another saddled gray horse stood ready which I surmised was for my special prisoner.

The troopers looked more like a party of hunters than an army detachment, save for their campaign hats, boots, and weapons. Sergeant Hoffmeister explained that they wore trail worthy clothes while on patrol, saving their regular uniforms for garrison duty. It seems that the material used in making uniforms was not conducive to western campaigns and the harsh climates which they encountered. Each man wore a rough shirt and trousers; some of them even made of canvas. Like wranglers and herders, each wore a neckerchief loosely around his neck.

When we were all ready, Sergeant Hoffmeister gave the order to mount. The troopers formed columns of two. I rode beside Hoffmeister. Troopers were detailed to lead our pack animals and spare horse. Captain Lloyd stood on the porch of the headquarters building as we filed past. Salutes were exchanged between the sergeant and the captain. Quickly, we were out on the prairie headed north as we followed the contours of Crow Creek for some miles. Eventually, we turned in a more northerly direction.

Several days later, we crossed the North Platte River. We found no sign of Indians until the fifth day on the trail. We came across a small abandoned campsite, which by the remnants of their meal, we determined was a hunting party of about ten. We figured that they were less than a day ahead, moving in the same general direction as us. We followed their trail for several hours before they turned toward the west. The sergeant presumed they were headed toward Fort Laramie.

Finally, we reached a point that Sergeant Hoffmeister studied with careful attention. He turned to me and advised, "Marshal Stockton, here is where we part ways. Our detail is turning west to pick up the route back to Fort Russell." I nodded my understanding as we shook hands. I bid farewell to my companions of the past week.

I sat Chino and watched the cavalry patrol ride out of sight before taking up the lead rope to my pack animal and spare mount. It would be a lonely ride from this point.

Three days later, I came across a strange sight. It appeared to be the remains of some sacred ceremonial place. Stones were placed in somewhat of a circle with bison skulls painted yellow, red, and black.

Because of an eerie silence, I became wary of my surroundings. The hair on the back of my neck seemed to stiffen. I withdrew my Winchester from its scabbard, holding it at the ready. The only movement was a soft breeze that fluttered through the grasses and ruffled my bandana a bit. I decided this spot was not a place to linger, so I moved onward as quietly as a man with three horses can travel.

I was well into the northern Montana Territory riding within a ravine when the ears of Chino and the other horses ears pricked up. I halted immediately to listen with caution. Momentarily, I heard faint voices speaking in a tongue unknown to me. I dismounted and crawled to the edge of the ravine.

Luckily, I hid downwind from several buckskin clad riders, mounted on painted ponies, and passing within fifty yards of my position. I took note of their weapons: they carried repeating rifles as well as their usual bows and sheaths of arrows. A half hour later they were out of sight and I exhaled a long rush. I sure didn't want to enter into a scrap at this time. I waited another half hour or so before continuing my journey northward.

A few days later, based upon a crude map Captain Lloyd had drawn at Fort Russell, I suspected that I had reached Saskatchewan province in Canada. I was proved correct when a lone rider appeared in the distance.

I halted and sat Chino watching the rider approach. The rider turned out to be a friendly Indian who spoke a bit of English. He related that he was a scout for the *red coat pony soldiers* and was taking a message to a detachment out on patrol. I rolled us both a smoke and we jawed a bit. I asked, and he provided directions to Fletcher's Station, adding that it was only a few miles further to the northeast. I thanked him for the information and watched while he continued west.

I arrived at Fletcher's Station in the late afternoon and sought out a livery stable for my animals. The station looked as if it had been built as a fur trading post first with other buildings added in later years: a livery stable, a saloon, café, hotel, and a few small houses in addition to the Northwest Mounted Police building and jail.

I saw to my horses first, then taking my saddlebags, duffle, and Winchester, I made my way to the hotel. It wasn't much to speak of, but it had a bed in a small room and that would do me. I decided that the Judge's special prisoner could wait until I grabbed a hot meal and some badly needed rest.

The fare at the café was about what I expected: beef steak with fried potatoes and cob corn. The bread was freshly baked and the coffee was strong and black. After supper, I went to my room for the night and, I can say without hesitation, once my head touched that soft down pillow, I drifted off with Laura in my mind. I could almost smell her lightly perfumed hair, and feel her softness next to me. That was the last thing I remember until the early light of dawn filtered through the curtains of my room. I could smell bacon and eggs with coffee brewing.

"Time to get up," I thought, "have breakfast and see about that prisoner."

An hour and a half later, I stepped into the Northwest Mounted Police building. I introduced myself to the young red-coated law officer and produced the document saying that I was to take charge of a prisoner known as *Charley Westbrook*.

The corporal acknowledged my authority, then remarked, "We are sure glad to get rid of Charley. Be extremely careful. She'll keep you on your toes." Then, he disappeared into the cellblock to retrieve the prisoner.

I was dumbfounded. Was there something wrong with that statement? Did he say, "SHE will keep you on your toes?" My mind raced. "How deadly could a woman be to have required a Deputy U.S. Marshal to fetch her back to Denver? How would a woman murderer behave on the trail back?" Most importantly on my mind was, "How could any woman require extreme caution?"

The corporal returned soon enough to the office area with an attractive young woman in tow, hands cuffed behind her back like she was, indeed, real dangerous.

The young woman had long flaming red hair, piercing dark brown eyes, and a curvaceous figure that showed itself in spite of her manly attire. She was dressed in bibbed overalls with homespun grey shirt and brogans. A folded red Indian trade blanket hung over her left shoulder.

Charley Westbrook eyed me up and down with a sly smile. I wondered then if she was relieved to be out of that cell and into my custody.

She spoke, "I'm Charlene Westbrook. Folks just call me *Charley.* So, you are what's supposed to take me back to hang for killing that no account husband of mine back in Colorado?"

"Yes, ma'am," I replied matter-of-factly. Then I finished, "I presume that you can ride a horse."

"A horse?" she replied in astonishment. "I want to ride in a coach."

"You'll ride a horse," I retorted. "This ain't no picnic we're going to."

An hour later found the two of us mounted and on our way back to Colorado. She rode well considering that I had cuffed her left wrist to the saddle pommel, leaving her right hand free to guide the reins.

Chapter Four

Horses to Wyoming

As the days passed Laura Sumner and her wranglers continued to work the newly acquired range stock, breaking them to saddle. Laura's men divided into teams of three with each working a designated corral to break the wild horses. The air near the corrals filled with dust swirls, excited yells from the wranglers, and sharp squeals of bucking horses.

Laura and her foreman Judd Ellison scrutinized the animals to determine which would stay on the LS Ranch for breeding, further insuring a viable stock herd. Together they moved the selected animals into a separate pasture close in to the ranch headquarters.

Laura and Judd returned to the main corral to watch yet another horse being broken to saddle. Mike Wilkes, Laura's youngest wrangler, was on a steel grey mare and he was *riding high*. Mike worked his lanky frame in tune with the animal's rhythm, anticipating every movement the horse made and countering it with his own. His light brown eyes sparkled with delight as he successfully wore the wild one down.

Laura turned to Judd, "You taught him well, Judd. Mike's a real bronc fighter now. I'm glad we hired him."

Judd chuckled to himself a bit before replying, "It was touch and go for a while, but you are right, Miss Laura. Mike Wilkes is a born wrangler. He knows horses, and he loves his work."

Laura smiled at the pride in Judd's voice. Mike wasn't Judd's son or nephew, but the older, more experienced horseman enjoyed seeing this young man learn his trade. Judd, as well as the rest of the LS ranch hands, had taken Mike under their wings and taught him well.

A lone rider entering the ranch yard momentarily diverted their attention. Both Laura and Judd recognized him. It was Johnny Miller, the telegraph runner on his paint pony. He waved at Laura and headed toward the pair. Johnny dismounted with folded paper in hand and presented it to Laura as he mentioned matter-of-factly, "It's from Cole Stockton, and Mr. Hubbard, the telegraph operator, thought it important. He sent me to deliver it."

With a smile of appreciation, Laura took the message from Johnny. "Thank you, Johnny. Ride on over to the house, there's molasses cookies and buttermilk in the kitchen."

Johnny grinned widely, "Thank you, Miss Sumner. I always like delivering out here to the LS Ranch." Johnny took his pinto by the reins and led it to the house where he tied up at the hitching rack, removed his hat, and bounded inside for his special treat.

Laura opened the telegram and read it quickly. Her face turned somber as realization of the words permeated her thoughts. The message related that Judge Wilkerson had assigned Cole to escort a very special prisoner for the judge and that he would be away for more than three additional weeks on this assignment.

Laura closed her eyes and took a deep breath, shaking her head. Judd detected a bit of mist in her disappointed eyes as he looked at her questioningly, "Is there something wrong, Miss Laura?" She turned away momentarily, handing Judd the wire. She paused to wipe her eyes. When she turned back to him, Judd saw the emotion on her face.

"Judd, I was so wishing that Cole would be with us on our next journey. It's just disappointing, that's all. Don't worry, I'm all right. I know he has to do his duty, but sometimes, I just hate that damn judge. Sometimes, I just wish that Cole wasn't a lawman so he could be here with us all the time."

Judd hung his head for a long moment before replying, "Miss Laura, you know why he does it? There ain't no one better to put the fear of the law into them that would do harm to folks. Why, I heard tell that outlaws just have to hear his name and they shake in their boots. If that ain't true, it ought to be. Cole Stockton is the best man with a gun in this territory, and he has sworn to uphold the law. I'm mighty proud to know him, and I think that you are too. By Jove, just think about it. If the judge picked Cole for this assignment, then, it must be very important."

Laura forced a smile as if to affirm Judd's comments. The foreman somehow knew just what to say when she felt down and out.

"O.K., Judd. Tomorrow you and I will go into town. I've heard that an army remount purchasing team will be at the hotel for the next few days. They'll be looking for good animals and I think that we've got what they need. We'll check out their ideas of remounts, then see if we can swing a deal. I'm hoping that we can get at least twenty dollars a head."

Judd removed his hat and, while wiping the sweatband with his handkerchief, thoughtfully mentioned, "Well, if we play our cards right, we might cajole them into about twenty-five dollars a head." He grinned as his eyes met Laura's.

Laura cocked her head to one side for a second. "You know, Judd, you are right. We should bargain for the higher amount. We put a lot of work into training those horses. Thanks for the suggestion."

Mid-morning found Laura and Judd approaching Miller's Station with their mounts at an easy walk. Shops were open for business. Townspeople mingled to pass the time of day before going about their errands. The steady clanging of a hammer on iron announced that the blacksmith shop was busy. The aroma of fresh coffee and fried bacon wafted close to the café. At the far end of the lone dusty street, Talbot's General Store had several wagons and saddle horses in front. Farmers shopped for wares, while womenfolk stocked up on staples.

Friends waved greetings to Laura and Judd who smiled and returned the wave. A trip to town was just as much a social visit as it was a necessity to stock up on supplies. With miles between homesteads, most folks welcomed a trip to town in spite of the distance.

Laura and Judd pulled up in front of the hotel, dismounted, and looped their reins around the hitching rack. Then they stepped up on the wooden boardwalk at the entrance to the establishment. Laura took a long breath and exhaled. "Well, Judd, let's see if those army people made it here." She led into the hotel lobby with Judd on her heels.

"Good morning, Mr. Beal," greeted Laura as she addressed the small statured, somewhat balding hotel clerk.

Beal looked up at Laura over his wire-rimmed spectacles and smiled. "Good morning to you, Miss Sumner. How may I help you this morning?"

Laura was pleasant as she posed her question, "I wonder if you have army guests in the hotel. I heard there might be men who are looking for remounts. Have they arrived?"

Beal nodded his head, "Yes, Miss Sumner. They arrived late yesterday. Out of Fort Russell I understand." He leaned closer to Laura to speak in a low tone offering, "I overhead them say they could possibly use close to a couple hundred horses. You are known to have the best in the area so I'm supposing they will pay you a visit. They talked about going to area ranches to look over stock before making any offers. There are three officers who are having breakfast just now down at the café. I figure they should return shortly. Will you wait here for them?"

Laura responded quickly, "Yes, Mr. Beal. I think we'll just wait right here in your lobby for them. Thank you very much for the information." Laura and Judd settled in chairs facing the front door to watch for the officers.

A few minutes later, a captain and two lieutenants entered the hotel lobby and headed to the desk. Beal nodded a greeting to them before he motioned toward Laura and Judd, announcing, "Captain Dansforth, you have guests waiting to speak with you."

Dansforth turned to find Laura and Judd seated nearby. He smiled brightly as he observed the attractive ranch woman. Stepping forward to bow slightly, he spoke, "I'm Captain Dansforth. To what do we owe the pleasure of this visit, Ma'am?" The two lieutenants likewise acknowledged Laura.

"That's Miss, Captain. I'm Laura Sumner of the Sumner Horse Ranch. I understand that you may be looking to purchase some remounts for your cavalry outfits. I believe that I can provide the quality stock you need. The LS Ranch has the best trained horses in this area and at the moment I have at least three hundred to choose from. Would you be interested, Captain?"

"Why, yes, Miss Sumner, we are interested. Army specifications for our remounts must be met, and we must personally view the prospective animals before offering any purchase agreement. If your animals can fit the bill, we may be able to do business. Each animal must be from fourteen to fifteen hands, sturdy enough for mountainous terrain, and trained to saddle and rider. I might also add, that we have color specifications as well. Some of our companies are looking to be color matched with sorrel, bay, black, grey, chestnut, and brown. Would you have horses to match those specifications?"

Judd grinned widely as Laura laughed lightly, "Captain, all our horses are mountain bred. We can meet all of your specifications. Would you like to accompany us back to the LS Ranch for a first-hand look?"

Dansforth replied enthusiastically, "Yes, yes! Might you meet us at the livery in about an hour? We'll be pleased to accompany you to see your stock." He turned to his lieutenants, "Gentlemen, make ready for the trail. Roust out our mounts and be prepared to ride within the hour." The three officers took the stairs to their rooms to change into trail clothes.

Laura turned to Judd, "I think we're in luck. No one else in this area can provide as many horses as we can. In the meantime, let's stop in at Talbot's to check out the latest gossip."

* * *

An hour later, Laura and Judd met the army officers at the livery. Once mounted, Laura led out with Captain Dansforth beside her. Judd fell in beside the two younger officers. They made small talk as they rode the forty-five minutes to the gates of the LS Ranch. Dansforth commented on the beauty of the landscape, "This area is certainly a pleasant change from the rolling prairie of Wyoming. What made you settle here?"

Laura reflected a moment before relating the story of her Uncle Jesse. "I'd always wanted to raise horses, and I got my chance when Jesse willed this ranch to me. I have in mind to build the best horse ranch in the territory. I believe that we've now got the stock for a solid beginning."

Arriving at the ranch, Laura served coffee and sweet rolls before she and Judd escorted the officers around the ranch. Standing at the main corral, they watched Eli Johnson ride the final training to a young sorrel, putting it through various maneuvers. The veteran wrangler guided the animal with complete savvy. Task completed, he rode up to the gate, dismounted, and dropped the reins in a trail hitch. The animal stayed where he was.

Laura glanced at the captain and asked, "Would you would like to try the sorrel for yourself?" The Captain eagerly accepted. Entering the corral, he put boot to stirrup and swung into the saddle. The horse responded to his every direction. In a matter of minutes, he asked to ride it outside the corral. Judd Ellison swung the gate open.

Dansforth spurred the animal from a walk into a faster pace, and then to a gallop. At the ranch gate, he slid the sorrel to a turn and trotted back to the corral. The captain was duly impressed with the experience.

"Miss Sumner," he exclaimed, as he dismounted. "your people have done well. The stock you have here fits the bill for our remounts." He grinned somewhat deviously, "How much do you want for say—one hundred horses of which fifty will be bays, the remaining fifty can be any color. The bays will be delivered to Fort D.A. Russell. The other fifty will be delivered to Fort Laramie."

Laura returned the smile with her own calculating wiles, "That's not the procedure, Captain. You tell me how much you will pay and then, I'll discuss it with you."

Dansforth laughed heartily. "Alright, Miss Sumner, you got me pegged. We are prepared to pay twenty dollars a head for exceptional animals."

Laura countered with, "I think the cost will be thirty dollars a head. You've seen the animals, and had the pleasure to ride one. You know these horses are well trained. We can match your requirements for immediate delivery."

Judd watched Dansforth's eyes as he glanced back at the two lieutenants. They nodded approval ever so slightly. The captain appeared to be calculating figures in his head. He spoke firmly, "Alright, Miss Sumner. The bottom line is twenty-five dollars a head. That is, twenty-five dollars a head to include immediate delivery. Does that meet your expectations?"

Laura laughed gaily, "I think you just bought yourself one hundred remounts, Captain Dansforth."

* * *

Later that evening, Laura, Judd, Scotty, and Eli Johnson sat around the kitchen table sipping coffee as they looked over a hand drawn map of the Wyoming Territory. They began to lay out plans to drive a hundred head of horses up into the territory.

Laura spoke first, "Boys, I suspect that we'll be ready to move out in another two weeks. I'm thinking that we want to drive straight north for the first two days, then shift east a bit in order to skirt Denver. We will then head to Fort D.A. Russell at Cheyenne. Fort Russell, I understand, lies on the west side of Cheyenne. Have any of you been there?"

Both Judd and Eli nodded the affirmative. Judd offered a suggestion, "Miss Laura, we're talking a couple of weeks on the trail. There are dangers aplenty and we will need some extra help with this ride. Have you thought about who might stay here at the ranch while we make the drive? And, have you thought of how many additional men we might need in order to make the trip?"

"Yes, Judd, I have. First, I believe we should leave Scotty and Mike Wilkes for the daily chores. Laura paused a moment to look directly at Eli Johnson, "I think that you should stay here also, Eli. You have a good head on your shoulders. You'll be in charge while we're away. You know what needs to be done, and I trust you to see things through until we return."

Eli appeared disappointed at not going; however, he also knew that after Judd, he was the most experienced wrangler. He nodded to Laura, "I will do your bidding, Miss Laura."

Scotty acknowledged his role, "Yes, Miss Laura, we three will take care of the home ranch. Mike will be sorry not to go, but he is a good man and will do his best here."

"Now, for the details," Laura continued, "what do you think of my plan, Judd? Is that the best way to travel?"

Judd pondered the map for a long moment and then nodded affirmatively. "Yes, Laura, I think by-passing both Colorado City and Denver is a good move. We know that Cheyenne is pretty near straight north after that. I've heard rumor of raiders working the area in between Cheyenne and Laramie so we will have to keep our senses about us. Now, for the extra help, Laura, who do you have in mind?"

"Well, Judd. I propose that you and I should go to town tomorrow to see if there are out-of-work but horse savvy men who would like to earn a month's wages. I understand that the usual pay for a drive like this should be about thirty to forty dollars for the trip. In order to secure those we need, we might go a bit more, say—oh, about fifty dollars for the right men."

Judd nodded his approval, "Yes, Laura. We should find some good men. I wouldn't mention wages until we check them out, though. And—Miss Laura, like I said before, that's a long trip. We need to think about provisions. In other words, we all like good cooking so as to eat good."

"H-m-m-m, I understand what you mean, Judd. Any ideas on how to solve that problem?"

Judd's reply came quickly. "Yes, I do. Cattle drives have got their chuck wagons with a cook. We ain't big enough to hire a cook with wagon, so let's think about a cook who is also a packer. I'm thinking a mule packer who knows his stuff and can put together something besides beans and bacon. In fact, I heard some time ago that ole Jeb Wooten who lives in that old shanty just outside of town used to scout a bit and pack for the army. I believe he knows a bit about trail cooking. What do you think?"

Scotty rubbed his mid-section and chuckled robustly, "Well, I'm probably the best at knowing food and such. Suppose that I go to town with you two and talk to this old man." Momentarily, Scotty laughed loudly, "I've even heard tell that Wooten is as salty as they come. That's a sign of a good trail cook."

* * *

The next morning, Laura stepped out to the stables clad in a tan and navy striped shirt, denim jacket, Levi's, chaps, and black Stetson. A soft pale blue silk bandana hung loosely around her neck. As usual, her gunbelt was strapped around her slim waist in a knowing manner. Judd was saddled up and ready. The stocky Scotty had his steel gray ready to mount. Mike Wilkes stood with a saddled Mickey waiting for Laura. She slid into the saddle, "Alright, boys, let's see if we can find some good prospects."

As they neared Miller's Station, Judd mentioned to Laura, "We should first check at the general store for word of local men looking for work. Next, go to the livery corrals. Most wranglers and drovers usually check in with the town corral for word of employment. They might also inquire at the stagecoach depot and general store for notices before looking up a cool mug of beer. I'll take casual notice at the saloons and express office."

Laura nodded, then announced, "And, I'll take the general store. I'll meet you at the livery corral in half an hour, Judd. Scotty, ride over to see our friend Jeb Wooten to make him an offer. I do hope he is game for the trip." Scotty peeled off from the two, riding directly to the far edge of town and Jeb's place.

Laura pulled up in front of Talbot's General Store, dismounted, then looped Mickey's reins round the hitching rack. She stepped upon the plank walk, then made her way into the store.

The cracker barrel crowd sat in wooden chairs near the center of the store by the potbellied stove. At Laura's approach, the four wise old men glanced at her and rose as one, "Good morning, Miss Sumner."

Laura smiled as she returned the greeting, "Good morning, gentlemen. I thought that I would seek your advice this morning. I've been awarded a contract to deliver some remounts to the Wyoming Territory and I was wondering if you have knowledge of experienced horsemen looking for work."

The men looked to each other only to shake their heads to the negative. John Taylor remarked, "No, Miss Sumner. We've not seen nor heard of anyone looking for horse work lately. But, we'll pass on your words iffen we do."

"Well, then, have you heard any news of the trails to Cheyenne and points north?" asked Laura.

Jacob Newton stroked his gray whiskers a bit before commenting, "I seem to recall a passerby telling of a rustler gang operating somewhere north and west of Cheyenne. But, I don't recall any more details."

Laura pondered that statement since it was virtually the same comment Judd Ellison made the previous evening. The thought crossed her mind that it would be nice to have Cole Stockton along on this drive. Quickly, she erased that thought. Cole was out of the question and this drive could not wait for one man, even if his name was Cole Stockton. The drive would commence in two days hence.

Laura bid farewell to the general store regulars and stepped out into the street to see Judd riding toward her. She looked inquiringly at him and he shook his head "No." Laura mounted Mickey, then the two of them rode to the livery corrals where they found three men sipping coffee and smoking hand rolled cigarettes. They dismounted, tied up to the corral bars, and approached the men.

The three men stood as Laura and Judd approached. Judd Ellison opened the conversation, "Any of you men looking for horse work? This here is Miss Sumner, owner of the LS Ranch. We'll be making a drive to northern Wyoming Territory and have need of a couple extra hands for a month's work. Might you be interested?"

The youngest of the three sat back down grumbling to himself and rolled another smoke. Judd looked sternly at the fellow and said with authority in his voice, "You got a problem there, pard?"

The man looked up at Judd and announced, "Yah, I do. I don't work for no woman."

Judd continued in a loud voice, "That's alright, sonny. We don't need you anyway." The young man gave a sour look, and turned his gaze away.

"Now, what about you other two fellers?" inquired Judd. "Do you have something against working for a lady?"

The other two men shook their heads to the negative. The tallest of the two pushed the brim of his Stetson back with his thumb and smiled. "I'm Jack McEntyre, most folks just call me Slim. I've been riding the grub line for a while and darned sick of it. Yes, I'd take working a horse herd to Wyoming. My experience is mostly wrangling the remuda for cow drives and I liked it a lot. I do a day's work for a day's pay. I'll go with you."

The second man, appearing mid-thirties, had a broad face with brushy mustache. He was neatly dressed with a pleasant smile. "I'm Jim Borden. I've mainly punched cows, but I've also fanned a couple of broncs in my time. I'd like to go with my friend Slim."

Judd sized both men up and glanced over to Laura. She nodded her acceptance. Judd addressed McEntyre and Borden, "You men are hired. The pay is fifty dollars for the drive. Get your trappings together and meet us at the far end of town in about thirty minutes. You have a space in our bunk house until we leave." Both men turned immediately to gather up their possessions then saddle up their mounts.

Laura and Judd made their way to their horses just as a rider on a dun horse approached them from town. Judd studied his mannerism. He was colored and looked every inch the epitome of an experienced ranch hand. The man pulled up in front of the pair. With tired looking eyes and a distinctly southern drawl, he stated, "I'd be looking for Miss Laura Sumner. Would you be her, Ma'am?"

Laura replied, "I'm Laura Sumner. What business do you have with me?"

"Well, Ma'am, I was just buying tobacco at the general store and asked about work in this town. An old gentleman told me that you was a-looking for riders to go to the Wyoming Territory. I knows my horses and I would like to go with you."

Laura cocked her head to one side and peered directly into the man's eyes as she contemplated his request. The animal he rode seemed well cared for which spoke a good deal of the man's character. He was polite and he seemed honest in his intentions. She spoke, "What's your name?"

The colored man spoke his name straight out with pride. "I'm known as Jeff—that is to say Jefferson Sutton. I was taught to read some, write some, and to do numbers."

Laura glanced to Judd. "Judd, I think we've found our third wrangler for the trip. Mr. Sutton, I pay fifty dollars for the drive. Do you accept the terms?"

Sutton smiled and nodded as he replied, "I do accept. I would be proud to work for you."

Laura addressed Judd and Jefferson, "Judd, give this man a five dollar advance on his wages. Mr. Sutton, I want you to buy yourself some new Levi's and a couple of new shirts. Meet us on the far end of town in fifteen minutes. You've got yourself a job. You will accompany us to the ranch. You have a place in our bunkhouse before we travel."

Sutton took the money offered, then rode directly to the general store. Within minutes he was back on his dun to meet the group. He rode behind Laura and Judd to the meeting place at the far end of Miller's Station. McEntyre and Borden were there waiting on them.

Momentarily, Scotty and Jeb Wooten on his own mule joined the Sumner Ranch entourage. Wooten was dressed in brogans, bibbed overalls, homespun shirt, and a worn floppy hat with the brim curled up in front. He spoke up, "Howdy, Miss Sumner. This feller Scotty has almost convinced me to join your expedition to Wyoming and back. But, I told him I need to haggle my wages. I don't take regular drover pay. If I'm to pack and cook, I bring my own mules, and my own packs. You provide for the supplies, but I'll do the buying. I like my tobacco, and I like my coffee. My wages are sixty dollars for the trip. Do you agree to that?"

Laura looked into the man's eyes, then spoke to him in a business-like manner. "I accept your terms for employment, Mr. Wooten." She next addressed Judd, "Write out a note to Mr. Talbot at the store that Mr. Wooten is to purchase supplies for our trip, putting the bill on my account."

A few minutes later, Laura handed Jeb the note, "Mr. Wooten, take this note to Mr. Talbot to buy your essentials. Be ready to travel on the third morning from now. We're going to Wyoming."

Chapter Five

The Trail to Colorado

Riding through the Montana Territory with a woman in tow could not have been further from my favorite pastime. Word had it that General Custer's outfit finding gold during the Black Hills Expedition the previous year had stirred up Sioux hostilities.

Such a discovery triggered a gold rush to the Dakotas. Reports of prospectors scalped by numerous Indian factions made for chilling stories. Newspapers sales peaked as details of mutilation became front page fodder. Still, more prospectors arrived, undaunted in their quest to get rich from Black Hills gold.

Tales of people slaughtered by tribes in other areas also circulated. True or false, the mere mention of Indian warfare put fear into settlers and pilgrims alike. Images in the mind of a lone rider or a homestead preyed upon by wild savages could unsettle the most steely-determined man.

In our case, two people on horseback with a packhorse, especially with one a woman, lent open invitation to some unwanted company. I had justly decided to travel with that notion in the back of my mind.

Charley stayed quite sullen during the first day or so of the trip. Actually, I found that fact much to my liking. Toward the end of the second day, we made camp in a small draw sheltered by a stand of pines. I took the cuffs off Charley then as I saw no need for her to remain shackled while camped. She cautiously looked at me with her big brown eyes. There was a certain reflection in them. It was the look of a need to talk, but yet uncertain trust.

I'd seen that same look before on women—just before they put me on the spot, and I grew leery of what she was contemplating. She reached down, picked up her blanket and drew it around her shoulders watching intently while I built a small fire. The coffee pot came next. While it brewed, I put together a meal of fried potatoes, beans, crisp bacon, and trail biscuits.

We ate slowly, savoring each morsel. Charley continued to watch my every movement. I felt scrutinized for something. Finally, she spoke for the first time since we left the Northwest Mounted Police station.

She looked me straight in the eye and said, "I done it, Marshal. I shot Frank with his own shotgun." Then, she looked upward into the vast star-filled sky for a long minute. I watched her in silence. When she looked back, our eyes met. Again, she spoke, "It wasn't the way you think, Marshal. Frank drank a lot. He would come home all drunked up, and beat me."

Her voice wavered then, and she hung her head for a moment to regain her composure. She bit her lip a bit, then continued, "He always said that it was my fault that he lost at cards, my fault that he drank so much, my fault that our small farm was failing." Charley stopped again to take a deep breath and stare into the fire for a minute or so.

I waited patiently while she took a few sips of coffee, then swallowed hard before continuing, "That night, he came home and beat on me again and again, Marshal. He rammed me into a table and then grabbed me by the hair and threw me to the floor. He stomped on me and then he went to the fireplace and got the iron poker. He staggered into the kitchen table. That dazed him for an instant. It gave me time to crawl to the corner behind the door for his shotgun. It was loaded. Enraged, he kicked the table out of his way. I told him to leave. He sneered at me, Marshal. He sneered at me, told me that he was going to break every bone in my body with that poker. He stepped forward and that's when I pulled the trigger. He jerked back hard and went down with a hole in his gut."

Charley's eyes glowed like hot coals as she finished her story. "I dragged myself to the pump and cleaned up the best I could. I guess it was then that I passed out and the rest is a blur in my memory. When I woke up, there was an old man and an Indian woman looking over me. It seems they stopped to water their wagon team at our trough and found me inside the house. They loaded me in their wagon with only the clothes on my back. The woman cared for me as we traveled north. I knew that I had to get away from Colorado so I traveled with the couple all the way to a village in Canada. That's where the Canadian Mounted Police found and arrested me."

My prisoner continued, "All the time I was traveling, I had bad dreams about Frank's brothers coming to kill me—to hang me. I know that family, Marshal. They are hard set to do an eye for an eye. Even now, I can feel them tracking me down." She paused as if to search my mind, then asked, "Can you blame me, Marshal Stockton? Can you blame me for what I done? I had to do it. I knew he would have killed me this time."

I studied this troubled young woman who showed no remorse. Her eyes were just as steady as any gunfighter I had faced in my time. An emotional chill ran up my spine as I answered her, "Charley, I don't make the judgments. I just uphold the law." I glanced into the dark sky before closing the conversation, "It's time to turn in. We've got a lot of distance to cover tomorrow and we need to be up to the travel."

Charley lowered her eyes, nodding her understanding. She moved to her blankets and rolled up in them, using her saddle as a pillow. I moved into my blankets across the fire from her with my Colt revolver close to hand. My horse Chino was my watchdog. He would alert me to any danger.

As I relaxed into slumber, I thought about Charley's story as my feelings crossed my mind once again. I don't hold with a man beating on a woman—never did, but it was not my call to make. My job was to deliver this woman to Judge Wilkerson. I would do my best to see it through.

* * *

As we broke camp the next morning, I recalled a statement Charley made the night before. Her words echoed through my mind that Frank Westbrook's brothers would try to track her down to do her in. A cold shiver came over me. The hair on the back of my neck pricked up. Yes, I felt uneasy. Out of intuition, I stepped away from the campsite to search our back trail. I turned my head to glance at Charley and asked, "Just how many brothers does Frank have?"

She looked up from gathering her possessions, "Three brothers. All three are trackers and good hunters."

"I'm glad to know that," I murmured softly under my breath. Now I knew what to expect should they happen to come across us on the trail.

Near mid-afternoon, we eased down into a long valley where in the distance a slow moving dark mass trudged toward us—buffalo. Now, buffalo meant bad news to me. Where there are buffalo, there are usually Indian hunting parties lurking nearby. I quickly angled us toward a pine-dotted slope.

No sooner had we disappeared into the pines than the herd of shaggy beasts churned into a thundering run up the valley. The earth shook with the might of a raging earthquake, and a cloud of dirt rose in the wake of the stampede. Buckskin clad hunters on painted ponies swooped in alongside the great brutes and downed several with either rifle, arrow, or lance.

"Oh, my God!" yelled Charley. Her horse shuddered a bit, stamping around anxiously. "Hold that horse, Charley!" I cautioned her. She pulled the reins back tightly. The pack animal jerked back on its lead rope, giving me warning to tie the lead rope snugly around my saddle horn. Chino set himself as the other horse pulled futilely against it.

Moments later, the cavalcade of hunters and hunted thundered past our position as if we didn't exist. I felt thankful we were unobserved and decided to go up the slopes to alter our route a bit. Now was no time for unwanted company.

Just before dusk, we came to a small clearing to find a burned out log cabin. Judging from the overgrowth of wild grasses, it had been years since occupied. Even with that thought, I felt that we hadn't put enough distance between us and the buffalo hunt.

We made a cold camp that evening. Canteen water and beef jerky would be the fare while our animals grazed on plentiful forage.

Charley unsaddled her mount and positioned her bedroll for the night while I unloaded the packs from the packhorse, hobbling both animals. I knew Chino would not range far.

Charley opened up a bit more while we chewed on tough trail jerky and sipped tepid water. "Marshal, I had those dreams again. They get more real each time I dream. I felt like Frank's brothers were close enough to reach out of the darkness and grab me. I'm scared.

I'm more scared of them than standing before that judge, even if it means a hanging."

"How do you know that they will find you out here?" I asked.

She looked at me with worry in her eyes, "The Northwest Mounted Police found me. They sent word to your judge. Maybe those boys found out through a friend at the telegraph office. Maybe they had a friend at the sheriff's office. I don't know, maybe, just maybe, they found out where I was by themselves. Besides, Marshal, there were a lot of people that saw us leave Fletcher's Station; just like there were a lot of people that saw the Mounties bring me to jail in irons."

Well, she had a point there and I pondered it. Even with spring in Montana, many nights still turned very cold and this night was no exception. We bundled up in our blankets looking forward to the warmth of a sunny morning. I slept fitfully with my own demons laughing in my face. At one point, I opened my eyes to a foreboding sense. Carefully, I looked around, but found nothing out of order. Still Charley's words worried me. Could the Westbrook brothers have been in the Canadian town when we left? Were they somewhere along the route behind us, or did they ride fast, determined to be somewhere ahead of us? I closed my eyes again as an uneasy sleep overtook me.

* * *

The morning of our fourth day of our ride back to Denver, I elected to relieve Charley of her cuffs. She looked at me questioningly. I responded to her puzzled expression, "Well, where would you go? I don't think you want to be by your lonesome in this territory." For the first time since we met, I detected the slight twitch of a smile. Her eyes radiated thanks.

A few hours later, we skirted a coulee only to discover a grim sight nearby. Four skeletons lay encircled yet grotesquely askew. Arrow shafts protruded from rib cages where flesh once lay. Skulls were smashed in. There was no doubt in my mind that scavengers of nature had feasted well.

A closer look revealed slash marks where scalps once were. Some two dozen empty cartridge casings lay strewn about, creating the scene of a fierce fight for life. I found no other clues as to who these people might have been. Charley shuddered at the sight as I grew increasingly more wary of our plight.

Nearly three hours later, three riders came toward us out of the distance. Charley watched them intently before announcing, "I recognize those men, Marshal Stockton. Those are Frank's brothers I told you about. They swore that I would pay for his death with my own. You'll never get me to that judge, Marshal Stockton."

"Take the lead rope to the packhorse Charley and stay behind me," I warned. Reaching back, I drew my Winchester, levering a round into the chamber. I waited until they were thirty yards from us before shouting the challenge, "U.S. Marshal. Don't come any closer."

The three men pulled up to look us over a long moment before replying, "We done found you, woman! Marshal, that woman kilt our brother, and we aim to see justice done. We don't believe the court will hang her for the killing, so we will just take her from you, and you can be on your way—that is, iffen you want to live, Marshal."

"The question is—which of you want to live," I retorted. "Turn about, or grab iron."

"They's three of us, Marshal. We gonna to get you good," and with that, the three as one reached for their weapons. That opened the ball.

I leveled my Winchester and shot the center one through the middle. He slammed backward off his horse. The other two spurred their mounts, spreading out to flank us. Molten lead whistled through the air. I could swear one almost burned my left ear. I expected to get hit at any second.

I led the one riding to the right side of me then squeezed off. My bullet grazed his side, causing him to wince in pain. Immediately, I swung round to snap a quick one at the brother to my left. I missed him, which caused a stream of curses from my lips.

He turned his horse to ride straight at Charley. As he leveled his weapon, I reached to my belt and within a split second, my Colt was in my hand firing once, twice, three times at almost point blank range. Somewhere in the midst of firing, his revolver discharged harmlessly into the air as his arms flailed and he jerked backward in the saddle. The next thing I knew, this brother slipped to the right. His animal galloped off with the man's foot caught in the stirrup, causing his body to bounce over the hard ground. That's a hard way to die in any man's language.

I turned to see the remaining brother holding his side as he leveled his revolver at us. He fired one round that whistled past my right cheek. With that, I shot him high in the chest, forcing him to jerk out of the saddle and drop hard on the ground. He rolled onto his stomach with pistol still in hand.

I dismounted a few yards away before walking up to him, Colt at the ready. Turning him over with my boot, I stuck the bore of my cocked revolver right into his face. The bewildered brother stared wide-eyed in disbelief that one man would stand against three in a gunfight.

"Who are you?" he asked with choked stammer. "Cole Stockton," I answered grimly.

"We never thought to ask," he replied. He coughed hard, blood flowing from his lips as his eyes clouded over in death.

I checked the first man down to find him stone cold dead as well. To search for the third man was out of the question. That horse could be a mile away by now.

Looking for Charley, I found that she had dismounted. She leaned against her horse shaking and in tears. I approached her quietly before touching her shoulder gently. She turned slowly, looked deep into my eyes for a long moment, then threw her arms around me, sobbing with her face buried against my shoulder.

Minutes ticked by. At last, she raised her tear-stained face to meet my eyes once more. Her lips quivered a bit as she mouthed the words, "No man has ever stood up for me before. I thought for sure I was dead. I owe you my life."

The thought hit me then that I had saved this woman from an agonizing death at the hands of her husband's kinfolk—but for what, a hanging at Judge Wilkerson's convenience?

I hated to do it, but all that gunfire within tribal territory might bring something that we didn't want. I dragged the two brothers together and left them like that. I also unsaddled their animals and shooed them off. I figured that any tribesmen who came about would want to catch the loose horseflesh rather than us. Taking their rifles, I smashed them against a boulder. No sense in leaving them for hostiles and we were burdened enough.

We mounted, then departed the area with haste. Several hours later, subtle changes in the landscape caused me to surmise we had crossed into the Wyoming Territory. I glanced at Charley. Her eyes were weary, her cheeks still showed tear stains, but her spirit was good. Relief filled her face.

Chapter Six

The Trail to Wyoming

Daybreak on the third day since hiring additional help for the remount drive, Laura Sumner stepped out to the porch of her ranch house clad in boots, Levi's, chaps, and dark blue shirt. A pale blue silk bandana hung loosely around her neck. Her Colt Lightning revolver rested in its holster around her slim waist. She carried Uncle Jesse's Henry rifle. Mickey was saddled, standing at the hitching rack.

Laura glanced around the ranch yard to see the wranglers forming one hundred and twenty-five horses for the trail to Wyoming. Twenty-five of them would be replacements should anything happen to any of the promised animals. She observed Tom Landon organizing the wrangler remuda. Laura's newest stallion, the black, was among them. She smiled widely, thinking about how she would put the black through his paces on this trip.

Laura set her duffle, saddlebags, and bedroll on the plank steps while she greeted Mickey, "Good morning, boy. Are you ready for a long ride?" Mickey seemed anxious to travel. Laura slipped the Henry Rifle into its boot, then tied the saddle bags, bedroll, and duffle on the back of the saddle. Looking up, she saw Eli Johnson, Scotty, and Mike Wilkes walking toward the main house.

"Good morning, Miss Laura," chorused the three when they were close. "We just come to see if there was any last minute instructions for us before you hit the trail."

Laura thought for a moment. Shaking her head, she replied, "No, boys. I trust that you all know what to do. We should be back within a month. Just keep this place running. Should anyone want to buy some horses, the price will be twenty-five dollars a head. I left a letter on the kitchen table appointing Eli in charge, authorizing him to issue any bill of sale.

Presently, Judd Ellison and the trail crew hazed the herd into the ranch yard. They halted the leaders in front of the house, pointing toward the gates of the LS Ranch. Laura put boot to stirrup and slipped into the saddle. Nodding to Eli with his home crew, she called out, "Take care, boys, and thanks."

Laura rode to the front of the trail herd to join Judd. She took a deep breath, exhaled, then loudly called out for all to hear, "All right, Judd. Let's take them to Wyoming." Judd raised up in his stirrups and gave the order, "Let's move out." He waved his right arm with the signal as he and Laura led the entourage through the gates, onto the road toward Miller's Station and the Denver stagecoach road.

An hour later they joined up with old Jeb Wooten and his pack mules. Jeb climbed aboard his riding mule on their approach. He wore his crumpled hat with an old cavalry campaign shirt and pale yellow bandana. A Springfield carbine sat in a half rifle boot at his side, along with a Civil War vintage Colt revolver at his belt. Jeb waved a greeting as Judd motioned for him to join the line with him and Laura. The cavalcade now complete, they crossed the main road to Denver and angled northeast toward the Colorado high plains.

Toward dusk, the trail riders turned onto the Great Plains keeping the Rocky Mountains to the west of them. Wranglers milled the horse herd to a halt while Jeb Wooten hobbled his mules, then set about unpacking his wares in anticipation of preparing supper. Shortly, he had a good campfire going. A pot of beans flavored with chunks of salt pork hung on a spit over the coals. A pan of corn bread sat on the hot stones surrounding the fire. A large coffee pot boiled at the edge. Jeb even had apples baking on the side.

Two wranglers rode slowly around the herd, maintaining calm as the animals grazed on tall grasses. Laura, Judd and the trail hands found a place to bed down for the night, placing saddles and bedding for comfort. The men lounged near the campfire as they compared tales of the day's travel.

After a time, Jeb finally announced in gravelly voice that supper was ready, "Here yah are, me buckos! Come and get it. And, don't expect niceties like baked apples for every meal, they is hard to come by."

The wranglers got to their feet, lining up at the fire with tin plate in one hand and cup in the other. Jeb dished out each plate similar in serving and poured coffee for each, "Eat it and like it. It will keep you alive," he grumbled.

As night came on, Judd searched the area for a forked stick. Finding one, he singled out the North Star and pushed the forked end into the ground at a slant with the single end pointing northward. "There's our marker for the morning," he announced, continuing with, "If we had a wagon along, we would point the tongue of the wagon toward the North Star."

After dark, the wranglers talked in hushed tones amongst themselves by the glow of the campfire. A couple of the men smoked their rolled cigarettes or puffed on a pipe. Jeb Wooten clenched a clay pipe between his teeth as he cleaned up the supper pots and pans. Each wrangler cleaned his own tins. Jefferson Sutton sat relaxed with a corncob pipe he had made himself.

The full moon's glow brought distant yipping, the distinctive serenade of the coyote. Laura shivered a bit as her thoughts turned to Cole Stockton. "Where is he? What is he doing on this evening?" She yearned to surprise him with the news of the black stallion. Selfishly, she wished that he was with them on this drive. "Damn that judge," she said softly under her breath before turning over in her blankets and closing her eyes.

Daybreak brought a quick breakfast of tortillas filled with left-over beans, bacon, and slivers of cheese. Jeb had made up a passel of tortillas before starting the drive. First, the wranglers saddled up, then grabbed a cup of coffee and a filled tortilla each. Laura and the boys got the herd moving slowly toward the north while Jeb cleaned the plates, repacked his mules, and doused the fire. He would catch up with the slow moving drive within the hour.

* * *

Three and a half days later, the herders spied thin distant smoke trails to the west of them against the snow-capped peaks of the Rocky Mountains. "There's Denver," remarked Judd pointing out the scene. "I suggest we angle yet more west a bit, then move parallel to the railroad into Cheyenne." Laura nodded approval of the idea, "Good thought, Judd. Let's do it."

Several miles further, they spotted dark movement with smoke spewing from the front of it—the Denver to Cheyenne train chugging its way to Cheyenne. "There's the train, Judd, turn them north," called Laura.

They spotted a sod house in the distance with a farm wagon to the side of it. Laura spoke quickly, "Judd, ride ahead to that homestead. See if the family is home and tell them of our herd. Inquire if they will allow us to cross their land. Ask what it takes for passage."

"I'll take care of it, Miss Laura," shouted Judd as he spurred ahead.

* * *

Judd Ellison rode slowly up to the sod house yard where he met a stout man clad in overalls. A young blonde woman wearing a full apron stood at his side and three tow-headed, blue-eyed children nearby. He noticed roughly an acre of freshly plowed furrows. The man leaned on his shovel at Judd's approach and issued a greeting with, "Guten morgen, sprechen sie Deutsch?"

Judd immediately thought, "Must be German. I don't talk that lingo," but undaunted, he said, "Good morning to you. Do you speak English?" He was pleasantly surprised when the man replied, "I am Konrad Hoffman and dis is mein frau Frieda. Jah! I speak Engliss gut."

Relieved, Judd related in as basic English as he could, "We have many horses with us. Where can we cross your land? Do you want payment to cross?"

Hoffman thought for a long minute. "You haf many horses?" "Yes", replied Judd, again asking, "Do you want payment to cross your land?"

The German nodded saying, "Jah! Dat be gut. Maybe you gif me von riding horse or tventy dollars?"

"One horse is worth twenty-five dollars," replied Judd, "That sounds reasonable. I'll be right back with a saddle horse and the ownership papers."

Judd turned and galloped back to Laura who immediately agreed to the offer. Judd directed Slim McEntyre to cut out one gentle animal from the surplus group while Laura wrote out a bill of sale.

Judd took the lead rope to the horse along with the document. Returning to Konrad Hoffman, he presented both to the farmer. The man looked over the gelding and nodded his satisfaction. He then advised, "You vil ride around my plowing, jah?"

Judd smiled and nodded, "Yes, we will ride around your plowing. Thank you. We wish you good harvest this season." He waved farewell as he turned his mount and rode back to Laura with the farmer's wishes.

The herd swerved westward to round the edges of plowed fields. Farmer Hoffman watched as the trail drive paid mind to his request, then faded into the horizon.

Two days later, Laura's trail herd came upon the remnants of an Indian village. Laura, Judd, and Jeb Wooten sat their mounts and surveyed the scene. A few lodge poles stood erect here and there yet markings in the earth told of many lodges. Jeb handed Judd the lead ropes to his pack mules, then rode slowly around the remains of the encampment. Momentarily, he dismounted and rummaged around what appeared to be a trash pile. He seemed to find something of interest and examined the object more closely. He motioned for Laura to come forward.

Jeb turned to Laura to show her what he had found. It was a crude carving of a bison. "Some child lost a toy," he exclaimed. He glanced about only to spot something on the ground a bit further from where they stood. He walked over and picked it up. Nodding his understanding, he also showed this artifact to Laura. This leather appeared to be a piece of worn moccasin. The old man studied the markings on it before speaking, "Cheyenne is my guess. I think we have come across an abandoned southern Cheyenne campsite. They are long gone from here. This camp is several days old."

Laura nodded, "Thank you Mr. Wooten, your experience is greatly appreciated."

Wooten reclaimed his packers from Judd, "I suggest that we drive around the outside of this camp area. That would show a bit of respect should any of the tribe return to the site."

Laura agreed. With Laura and Judd in the lead, they skirted the campsite and once again headed north. As a matter of habit, Wooten took notice of the direction that the Cheyenne trail led. He mumbled to himself, "Looks a lot like they are headed to the mountains, but you never know. They might turn again somewhere."

* * *

Several days later, wisps of smoke appeared in the far distance. Judd remarked, "Well, Laura. That must be Cheyenne coming up. Fort Russell is on the west side of town. I suggest that we cross the rail tracks here so we don't have to drive through town to get to the fort." They turned west and within two miles crossed the iron ribbons of progress.

As the entourage neared the fort, Judd advised Laura, "That would be Crow Creek to the left of the fort. I suggest that the boys water the herd there while you and I go find the quartermaster to see about delivery of the first fifty animals."

Laura responded, "I'm with you, Judd." Tom can take charge while we make arrangements." Judd signaled to Langdon to hold the herd at the creek.

Laura and Judd rode forward to the main gate of Fort D.H. Russell. A post sentry directed them to the quartermaster building. They tied up in front of the long wooden structure and entered the building. A bespectacled gray-haired sergeant looked up from his paperwork to inquire of their business.

"I am Laura Sumner of the LS Ranch in southern Colorado. We have a written contract to deliver fifty remounts to Fort Russell. Where do you want us to put them? And, who do we see for payment?" inquired Laura.

The sergeant replied, "One moment, Ma'am. Let me get my captain."

The sergeant stood and then left through a side door. Momentarily, the door reopened and Captain Dansforth stepped into the outer office. He smiled a greeting to them, then welcomed Laura.

"Miss Sumner, it's good to see you. You made good time in getting here. We are anxious to get your horses. But, first, we must inspect the animals to ensure that you brought the correct ones."

Laura scowled a bit. The thought crossed her mind, "Well, it seems like the army doesn't trust their contractors, or is it just this one absurd authoritarian?" She shrugged it off with "I guess that it's just good business to insure your investment. I'd do the same."

Dansforth turned to the non-commissioned officer beside him, "Sergeant Beamis, notify Corporal Todd to get the reception corrals ready. We'll be receiving remounts shortly."

"Yessir!" replied the sergeant and took his leave through another door to the warehouse. The captain then turned to Laura and Judd, "Walk with me to the stables while I get my mount. I'll accompany you to the herd for inspection."

Laura and Judd took their horses in tow. They walked with Dansforth to the cavalry stables, where an orderly saddled the captain's mount for him. Once mounted, the three rode to Crow Creek where he took his time selecting the desired remounts for Fort Russell. They made small talk while Laura rode around the herd with him. "As a matter of curiosity, Miss Sumner, and your being from southern Colorado, do you know a U.S. Marshal Stockton?"

Laura was taken back at that statement. "Why yes, Captain Dansforth, I do know Marshal Stockton. Cole is a very good friend of ours. Why do you ask?"

Dansforth noted Laura's use of first name, then related, "Well, he was through Fort Russell about two weeks ago. He left with one of our patrols headed north into the Montana Territory."

Laura couldn't hide her curiosity. "I had no knowledge of that, Captain. Thank you for the information. Do you know his destination?"

Dansforth thought for a moment, "No, I'm sorry. I don't know where he was going, but his mission seemed secretive and urgent." Laura's mind raced with questions.

Both remained silent with their respective thoughts while they continued to circle the herd. When the captain was satisfied with his selection, he requested, "Miss Sumner, if you will have your men drive those fifty to our corrals behind the quartermaster building, I'll issue your draft for payment."

An hour later, Laura and Judd returned from the fort to the wrangler's creek encampment with payment in her pocket. After unsaddling Mickey and settling her bedroll in a comfortable place, she got a tin cup of coffee from Jeb and sat down on the ground next to her foreman.

"Judd, I found out something about Cole's whereabouts. Dansforth told me that Cole was here at Fort Russell just two weeks ago. He left here with a cavalry detachment headed for the Montana Territory. What could that mean?" related Laura.

Judd turned to face her, "I don't know, Laura. Maybe the prisoner he had to pick up is in Montana. That's a mighty long way to go to pick up a fugitive. There must be something out of the ordinary about that person."

Laura lowered her eyes from Judd's view while she pondered his statement. She thought of the other part of Dansforth's revelation, that Cole's presence was secretive and urgent. What could that mean? What was Cole's real purpose in going to the Montana Territory? She would need to think on that a while.

The LS Ranch group rested for one more day at the Crow Creek encampment. Jeb and Laura went into Cheyenne to replenish dwindling staples for the trail. They were running low on Arbuckles coffee, potatoes, apples, bacon and ham. Browsing the store, Laura found a beef roast. A smile crossed her face as she envisioned how her men would receive this supper treat. Her wranglers would eat well before resuming the trail the next morning.

The next morning, Judd outlined the trail herd's next destination over a Jeb special breakfast of scrambled eggs, potato, and bacon strips in a flour tortilla with hot sauce. Judd explained that Fort Laramie was situated on a bluff overlooking the Laramie River. "The original fort was built as a trading post." Judd related, "The army took it over and moved it to the present location."

Laura added her concerns, "We've got a hundred miles further to complete our contract. This leg of our journey holds even more dangers. I understand that Fort Laramie units are continually engaged in the pursuit of hostile Indian bands. We must keep a sharp look out."

After breakfast, Laura and Judd again took the point and led out toward the north. Initially, Laura and her wranglers found the landscape to be vast rolling prairie with long slopes that rose and diminished. Occasionally, there were tree-dotted hills. Periodic Wyoming winds brought fine sand, insects, and intermittent mud splotches into their faces. Further into the Wyoming Territory, the scene changed to more pronounced hills, ravines, and stands of hardwood.

Just prior to sundown of the first day out of Fort Russell, they crossed Lodge Pole Creek and arrived at Horse Creek. Judd and Laura chose to cross the creek and make their evening camp on the north side. Trees and low foliage lined the creek. Grass was plentiful, and the water was cool and clear. The wranglers situated the much smaller herd of horses for a night at this near perfect campsite.

The beauty of the woods and crystal clear water brought thoughts of a relaxing plunge into the creek. The drovers were first to do just that. Laura walked a bit upstream around a bend where she enjoyed the privacy of tall bushes. Judd Ellison planted himself as guard between Laura's private bath and the downstream noise and rowdy antics of her boys.

Later, the trail drivers enjoyed a sumptuous beef stew and biscuits. After supper, the wranglers rolled up their homemade smokes and relaxed while Jeff Sutton sang plantation spirituals, accompanied by the multi-talented Jeb Wooten on his harmonica. Somewhere in the distance, dogs-of-the-plains yipped their contribution to the chorus.

The dark sky twinkled with millions of stars as the campfire embers provided a soft glow. Wranglers settled down in their bedrolls, and soon, the only sound was the hushed song of the night watch wrangler soothing the souls of both man and beast. Periodically, the night guard placed another stick into the fire to keep it alive.

Morning brought the aroma of bacon, eggs, and boiling coffee. Jeb had a few potatoes baking in the coals with tortillas warming along the side of the fire. The old man's time near the border with

Mexico brought a love of tortillas with savory filling. He served them often. Wranglers rose, packing their gear, selected their mount for the day, and saddled them. Laura chose to give Mickey a break and to ride the black stallion on this day.

Morning routines were set. After a quick breakfast of Jeb's tortilla wraps with hot sauce, the wranglers went to saddle and took up their positions. Laura and Judd again rode the lead with the remount herd behind them. The wranglers filled the outrider and drag positions. Jeb Wooten would strike camp, then hurry forward to catch up with the drive.

The lead duo kept the pace slow for the first couple of hours until Jeb joined them. After re-uniting, the group picked up the pace. At noon they halted an hour for rest and cold lunch. Jeb quickly assembled sandwiches of bread with thick slices of cheese and ham.

The first hour in the afternoon drive brought a sudden Wyoming wind that forced the herd to slow to a snails' pace. The wranglers fit bandanas to their faces, pulled hat brims down, and leaned into the wind in order to see their direction. Laura had planned to make camp within half a day's drive of Fort Laramie that evening, but now it seemed doubtful.

Just as quickly as the wind rose, it died down. Laura's hopes for the close evening camp seemed attainable. Her black stallion continued responding well to her every command. She loved the feel of the animal. The black's stamina was unsurpassed. The ranch woman glanced back at the wrangler remuda. Mickey seemed to enjoy his unburdened travel alongside stable mates. Laura smiled a bit, then looked over at Judd.

Judd had a strained, even puzzled look on his face. At that moment, Jeb Wooten trotted his packers up close to Judd, then loudly announced, "I got a bad feeling, Judd. To tell the truth I've been a bit worried for the last hour or so. I got this feeling that we aren't alone. I tell you, I've got feelings that something is wrong here."

Judd turned back to Laura to relay Jeb's concerns. He included his own apprehension as well, "Laura, I've had those same feelings. There's something coming. Something bad is coming!" Laura closed her eyes for a moment to collect her thoughts. A fearful shudder shook her body.

They led the remount herd down a long slope, then across the clearing toward the opposite incline of trees and underbrush. Six riders appeared out of nowhere in front of them. The surly men each bore a rifle in hand. In an instant, gunfire broke out from the rear of the herd. Before Laura, Judd, and Jeb could respond, the remount herd surged forward in an all-out run with animals bursting past them.

Simultaneously, the six men in front of Laura and her two lead men split and leveled their rifles at them.

"Oh my God!" yelled Laura. "Raiders! Watch out, Judd!"

Judd Ellison had drawn his rifle from its scabbard. Jeb Wooten whipped his carbine up, took aim at a raider and before he could fire his weapon, a bullet hit him square in the mid section causing the old man's body to slam backward off his mule. The other two pack mules bolted into a dead out run in opposite directions. Their packs loosened, allowing utensils and food supplies to spew over the prairie as the two mules sought safety. One mule bolted some thirty yards before a raider shot it dead. The other brayed loudly in pain as he went down with a broken leg.

Laura moved to draw her Colt Lightning when a rifle round seared through her body causing her to jerk hard in the saddle; however, she kept her balance. Her left hand fell immediately to the wound as she screamed out in pain. Blood seeped through her fingers. Panic swept over the woman as she looked down at her wound before she lurched forward against the neck of the black. The stallion jumped straight into a ground-eating run amongst the surging mass of remounts.

Nausea churned inside her stomach as Laura fought to stay astride her mount. Darkness filled her mind. Instinctively she reached for her lariat. With all her strength, she looped the rope around the pommel of the saddle as well as her body, tying herself into the saddle as she fought off dizziness. Her last thought was of Cole Stockton, "Cole! Where are you?"

Laura flopped like a rag doll as she lost consciousness and fell forward against the black's neck. The remount herd and remuda ran full out with wranglers fighting for their lives. A full-fledged stampede evolved.

Minutes ticked by before the black with its tethered burden turned out of the herd and galloped toward an embankment lined with trees. The stallion surged into the timber and down the other side and then splashed quickly across a stream. The black climbed the second embankment, never losing his footing. He galloped onward into the falling dusk.

Back on the prairie, Judd Ellison's horse had been killed. Thrown headfirst onto the prairie, Judd had dislocated his left shoulder. His rifle lay empty a few yards from him. Judd drew his revolver and fired four shots at the retreating raiders who drove after the remount herd in the distance. He waited in pain for a few minutes, then rose to his knees to look back at the bloody scene behind them. He thought, "Laura! Laura! Where are you?"

Judd's eyes searched in vain for Laura. He stumbled upon Jeff Sutton who lay face down in Wyoming dirt with a bullet in his right shoulder. Further back, Tom Langdon lay dead, trampled by the herd after his mount tripped and fell into a wall of horseflesh. Slim McEntyre would speak no more. He lay dead with a bullet to the heart. Jim Borden had been catapulted to the ground as someone had shot his horse from under him. Judd found him tending to George Latham who lay unconscious with a bullet to his middle.

Silence swept over the Wyoming landscape. Three of Laura's men needed burial, and four sought to rejoin, to stand together for survival. One of them was missing. Where was their Boss Wrangler? Where was their beloved Miss Laura?

Chapter Seven

Fort Laramie

Charley and I traveled without incident for the next day and a half. In the early afternoon at the bottom of a long slope, we came across three burned out wagons. They appeared to be the remains of a freighting outfit.

The contents of the wagons, farm implements, lay strewn over a considerable area. Shovels, picks, and hoes must have been on their way to a general store. There were empty tins that once held canned meats and fruits for mercantile shelves. One crate had been axed open with its contents missing; however, remnants of cloth gave me reason to believe it had been clothing or yard goods.

Indians would certainly take all they could use with them. They would especially take any livestock. I took note of the general direction the marauders took on their departure.

As I suspected, three teamsters lay nearby in a defensive circle. They were bristling with arrows, stripped of clothing, scalped, and limbs slashed. This death scene was a definite warning to all who would cross into the land of the Cheyenne. The Cheyenne were often referred to as the *cut-arm people,* due to their practice of slashing body parts of their slain enemy.

Charley helped me bury the hapless freighters. Her face was ashen and she clenched her teeth, but she was more than ready to render this humane task. After doing for the deceased men, we mounted and I took up the lead rope to our packer. I decided that we were within a close distance of Fort Laramie. The soldiers there would want to know about this incident. I left with a couple of arrows. Someone at the fort would know what tribe carried such markings.

We camped that evening along the North Platte River. I figured that following the river downstream the next day, we would reach the fort sometime around late morning. Charley volunteered to do supper for us, and even with meager fixings, she proved a much better cook than me. Even the coffee seemed tastier.

We talked a bit over our meal, "Marshal, I ain't never seen anything like that wagon killing before. I've heard some about it, but never seen it. I just couldn't imagine anything like that." She closed her eyes as her body shuddered a bit.

"I've seen enough like that," I admitted, "and, still, it's not something you get used to. Try and put it out of your mind." Charley nodded, but I could tell that the scene would haunt her for some time to come.

* * *

True to my estimation, Charley and I rode into Fort Laramie before noon the following day. There was no stockade. The buildings formed a quadrangle around a parade field where troopers engaged in drills and details.

Sentries gave us the once over as we approached them, especially Charley. I identified myself and we were directed to the post headquarters building where I could make my report to the adjutant. I grinned as we rode to the headquarters. It would take a week for the sentries to wipe those silly grins off their faces from ogling Charley, but they were no threat to her.

Tying up at the hitching rack in front of the headquarters building, I motioned for Charley to wait in a chair on the porch. The two sentries at the door could delight themselves for a few minutes while I related the news about the freighter outfit.

After identifying myself, I gave preliminary observations to the sergeant at the desk. He disappeared into an office only to quickly return to usher me in to see the commanding officer. Colonel Martin greeted me with, "Marshal Stockton. We know of you. I understand that you have information about an Indian raid not far from here. Is that correct?"

I acknowledged that fact, and produced the arrows I'd taken removed from the dead freighters. "These are from the three bodies we found. I suspect that they are Cheyenne, but your people will know definitely. The tracks of both unshod ponies as well as the wagon teams led off toward the mountains."

After relating all the information that I had, I followed the colonel to the outer office. He then directed the adjutant to form a cavalry detachment to ride to the location and pick up the trail.

Just then, a lieutenant entered the office and inquired of the NCO on duty, "Sergeant Norton, have we had any more word from Fort Russell of Miss Sumner and our remounts? We were expecting them sometime yesterday."

At Laura's name, I suddenly turned my interest to the lieutenant, "Did you say Sumner? Laura Sumner is on her way here with remounts for Fort Laramie?"

The officer turned to face me with a questioning look on his face. Colonel Martin nodded to the lieutenant, "It's all right, Lieutenant Saunders. This is U.S. Marshal Stockton. You may relate your situation to him."

Saunders replied, "Yes, Marshal Stockton. Miss Laura Sumner is to deliver fifty remounts to us. In fact, Fort Russell telegraphed us that they left there with an estimated arrival here at Fort Laramie sometime yesterday. We've heard no word since."

Suddenly, a foreboding feeling came over me. By all appearances, and I hoped that I was wrong, Laura and her party had run into trouble somewhere between Forts Russell and Laramie.

I responded to the information with, "I see. Colonel, do you have any further need of me? Miss Sumner is a personal friend of mine and I think that I'd better go looking for her and your remounts."

Colonel Martin added his concern, "No, Marshal. You've provided us with valuable information. Go and find your friend and our stock." We shook hands farewell and I went out to the porch to fetch Charley.

"Charley," I said in a barely audible tone, "we are going to take a detour. I'll explain on the trail."

We mounted, and with packhorse in tow, rode out of Fort Laramie headed south. Once off the confines of the fort, I explained our change of plans. "Charley, a friend of mine is on the way this direction from Cheyenne. They were supposed to be at Laramie yesterday. We are going to look for them. I fear that some ill fate has happened upon them."

Charley sensed my concern. After time on the trail with me, we had learned a good bit of the other's character.

Toward evening, we made a cold camp in a small grove of trees. Charley understood that a fire in this territory, regardless of how small, might bring unwanted visitors. We settled down for the night with nothing more than canteen water and jerky to sustain us. I drifted off to a fitful sleep wondering if tomorrow would bring a joyful reunion or dark misery.

* * *

The two of us were in the saddle with first light, headed in the direction of Cheyenne. I rode with ever increasing wariness clouding my mind. I continually searched the horizon before us, looking for movement that resembled a herd of horses. Then, after some four hours into the ride, a group of five riders emerged from a tree-lined slope and turned toward us.

I brought our three animals to a halt while I studied the approaching group. The rough men were not familiar to me. I turned to Charley, "Take the lead rope to the packhorse and stay behind me."

I scrutinized them closely as they drew nearer, taking special note of their mounts and the manner in which they wore their guns. There was something familiar about the black horse one man rode.

The group pulled up about ten yards in front of us and just sat there looking at us—rather, they were looking and leering at Charley. I'd seen that look before, and the way Charley was fidgeting, she'd seen that look before as well. It was a look of sheer lust.

I didn't like the looks of this bunch. I knew that black horse. Without thinking, I blurted it out, "Mickey!" The stallion's ears pricked up, as he started toward me, but the dour-faced rider kept him in check.

"Mister," I growled, "you've got just ten seconds to explain how you come by that animal before I shoot you off it."

The five looked at me and grinned. One man cocked his head to one side, narrowed his eyes, "He got that animal same way that we are fixing to take your horses—and that woman."

I didn't wait for them to show me. I drew and started shooting—the Devil take the slowest. The first man down was the one riding Mickey. I burned his left side good, and the impact of that

.44 caliber slug ripping along his flesh toppled him from the saddle. I wanted him alive.

Gunsmoke filled the air as revolvers discharged quickly in a melee of rearing and fidgeting mounts. I fired blankly into the group, then drew my second Colt from behind my back, methodically lining up and shooting two more men. Both jerked out of the saddle to hit the ground without moving. The remaining two turned tail and rode off like Satan himself was on their heels.

Charley was quite calm this time. She had been through this type of circumstance with me before and she knew my capabilities in a gripping situation. She held tight to our wild-eyed pack animal, preventing him from escaping the scene.

I dismounted to walk up to the wounded man who had been riding Mickey, then turned him over. When I grabbed him by his shirtfront, he winced with pain. Blood spread along his side as he instinctively put his hand over the wound to stop the bleeding. I placed my Colt right up against his forehead, cocking it. The sliding hammer of cold steel against steel has a way of making a man sweat. This was no exception.

"Like I said before, you've got ten seconds to tell me where you got that horse or so help me I'll blow your brains out."

He quickly stammered out his explanation about the gang of twenty or so riders who attacked a horse herd, "We hit a cavalry remount herd two days ago. Some of the wranglers were wounded," he said, "but we left them out on the prairie. We didn't stop to kill them. I caught this horse up with the herd, and liked the looks of it. I decided to keep it for myself."

"Bad mistake," I said. "I am Cole Stockton, Deputy U.S. Marshal. You are under arrest for rustling and attempted murder. You'll come peaceably along to guide me to where you hit that remount herd or I'll leave your dead carcass for buzzard bait."

I turned to Charley, "I need your horse, Charley. You will ride the black. His name is Mickey and he belongs to a friend of mine. Get me those handcuffs from my saddlebags. I have need of them."

Charley sensed my need of her assistance as she quickly responded to my requests. After handing me the handcuffs, she cautiously approached Mickey. After several minutes of soft words and gentle strokes to the shaken black horse, Charley took up the lead rope on the packhorse then mounted Mickey.

After seeing to the outlaw's wound, I mounted him on the spare horse, then cuffed his left hand to the saddle horn. Now, I faced the big problem. Laura wouldn't just let Mickey trail the herd unless she had an equal mount. They had been hit by rustlers. Some of Laura's wranglers were wounded, or worse yet—dead. If Laura wasn't with Mickey, she would be looking for him.

A fearful feeling wretched in the pit of my stomach, and I sensed the danger that Laura faced. These men were hard-bitten and lawless. They were just plain ugly mean men. It would take a man capable of meting out an equal share of meanness to deal with them.

"I've got to find her," I thought, "and—I've got to take these two with me." Another scene crossed my mind. "No doubt, the two that got away will be returning with help from the gang." I figured I'd already pressed my luck something fierce.

Once I got mounted, my wounded prisoner let me know the approximate location of the raid. I led out with the rustler beside me. He was sullen, but knew better than cross me with misinformation. Charley brought up the rear leading the packhorse. We wasted no time eating up the miles between us and the last known site of Laura's herd.

At near dusk I caught site of a slight wisp of smoke in the distance. Could it be a campfire?

I would have to be very careful in our approach. As we neared the campfire, I called out, "Hallo the camp!" A responding challenge answered my announcement, "Come forward and identify yourselves!"

The voice sounded familiar and I called out loudly, "U.S. Marshal, we are coming in!"

The anxious miles of riding brought slight relief—four of Laura's men, wounded, and horseless, huddled together. They stayed at the ambush site, in case someone like me came looking for them.

Laura's foreman, Judd Ellison, was among them. "Cole! We are damn glad to see you," he said. "We lost three of our men. They're dead. We don't know Laura's whereabouts. I believe that she was hit when the shooting started. She's on a good horse which leads me to believe that she made it away. They left us for dead."

Well, there it was—straight out. Laura was missing. Although Judd's account was brief, I envisioned the attack.

I had the wounded outlaw dismount, after which I cuffed both of his wrists in front of him. "Sit down over there by the fire," I commanded. The prisoner did as I bid. "Judd, this man is one of your raiders. He is the reason I found you."

Laura's men glared at him with venomous looks. I knew that they were just itching to get their hands around his throat to throttle him within an inch of his life. On a second thought, I instructed Judd in assuredly audible tones for the wranglers and prisoner alike to hear, "I need you to help guard him. And—he is not to be touched." That last statement brought low grumbles from the surviving wranglers. Judd understood exactly what I meant.

Looking at Judd, I asked, "Do you have food and water?" Judd shook his head negatively, "We've had nothing to eat for the past two days and water is scarce."

"Well, Judd, I brought a very good cook with me as well as a few vittles. The young lady with me is Charley. We've been traveling some together."

I turned to Charley, "Would you fix up a supper for all of us?" Charley smiled and nodded. Jim Borden moved to help her unpack the pack animal before moving it out from the immediate camp to hobble it. Charley set to work with coffee pot and frying pan.

Turning back to Judd I searched his weary eyes and assured him, "Judd, at first light, Charley and I will track down Laura. We will leave our pack animal with you, as well as most of the staples." He nodded his understanding.

Later, after a small but nourishing meal and some hot coffee, we all rolled up in blankets. Once again, I slipped into fitful sleep with Laura constantly on my mind. She kept calling out to me, "Cole, where are you? I need you. Come to find me!" I woke with a start as I mouthed the words, "Hang on, Laura! I am coming." I looked about me but all was silent.

Chapter Eight

Laura's Salvation

At daybreak, the wrangler camp was awake and waiting for Charley's version of beans, bacon, and biscuits. Coffee was on and the aroma beckoned to each of us. Soon, Charley and I would ride out to search for Laura. It was easy to see that the young woman appreciated the polite attention given her by Laura's wranglers.

When it was light enough to read sign, I spoke to Charley, "I'm going to track down Laura and I'd like you to come along with me. I may need some woman-type help." She readily agreed and the two of us saddled up our mounts.

We rode the outskirts of the remount herd path looking for tracks of a lone horse leaving the stampede. After half an hour, I found tracks of a horse headed fast away from the scene. I hoped that Laura was on that animal. After studying the situation, my gut feeling said that she was.

We followed the prints up slope through trees and thick brush. At times, I had to stop and look carefully in order to find clues for the direction. Tracking became more difficult. It looked a lot like the horse expected chase by the evasive movements that it made. It changed direction several times.

With the sun at high noon, we stopped for an hour rest. I passed the canteen and a piece of jerky to Charley. She silently took the fare, studying my eyes. A few minutes later, she spoke, "You really love this woman, don't you?"

I nodded a bit as I replied, "We've been through some rough times together."

"You're worried. It shows." she continued, "I never had a man worry over me like that. It might've made a difference, if I had known such a man." I looked into her eyes. This time, they held a certain softness that I had not seen before.

I nodded, "Yes, Charley. I reckon so."

Once rested, we were back on our mounts. Again, the trail became difficult to make out. During the afternoon I observed Mickey's behavior. Laura's horse seemed anxious about the landscape ahead of us. He made an effort move more quickly, but Charley kept him in check. I thought about how the stallion seemed anxious. I made my decision.

"Charley, give Mickey his head. Just take a loose rein with him and let him go where he wants. I think he may have scented Laura and he knows that we need to find her. Let him take us to her."

Charley nodded, "I think that you are right, Marshal Stockton. His pace is quickening."

Two days earlier, the black stallion sensed the weight shifting on his back and slowed to a walk. There was something wrong and it worried him. Laura was not guiding him anymore. Slowly, the black picked his way through yet another forested area of the Wyoming hills. Periodically, he stopped to listen for pursuit. None came.

The magnificent animal instinctively knew that a pasture of good grass lay ahead within reach of a cool stream. He carefully picked his way to the valley. Once there, he drank from creek then grazed on the tall sweet Wyoming grass nearby, oblivious to the limp figure tied to his saddle.

Periodically, the stallion's delirious burden rambled on with an incoherent voice that faded in and out. "Where are my wranglers? Are they all right? I h-u-r-t so badly. Cole? Is that you Cole? Come to find me Cole. Where are you Cole?"

Late morning of the third day since the savage attack on the herd, Laura Sumner lay slumped forward on the neck of the stallion. The animal moved in the tall grass along the creek.

The bullet that passed through her side caused loss of blood, pain, and periods of unconsciousness. Dried blood caked her side, gluing her shirt to raw flesh. Laura was in a daze, her breathing slow and shallow.

I watched as Mickey led up the next slope, then stopped for a moment, his head raised and nostrils flared against a soft breeze. Again, he moved forward down the slope and through yet another stand of trees to enter the clearing. Once again he stopped before shifting his head from side to side, searching. His keen nose caught a familiar scent.

Mickey moved toward the far end of the clearing. That's when I saw it—a black horse with what appeared to be a bundle on its back.

I urged Chino forward, fearful of what we would find. Charley on Mickey rode right beside me. We were near a gallop moving toward the black when he raised his head and looked straight at us. As he moved, the bundle on his back jolted.

Mickey suddenly stopped in his tracks and let out a loud squealing whinny. The black slowed to a stop, head raised with nostrils flaring. He seemed to shake with indecision on whether to run or stand.

Again, Mickey whinnied as he moved at a walk toward the black. I sat Chino and called to Charley, "That's got to be Laura on the black. Let Mickey take you closer. When you can, reach out to take up the reins and hold him. I don't think that he'll let me close to him."

I watched as Mickey broke into a trot. Quickly, he was beside the black muzzling Laura's limp form. The black stood still while Charley reached out carefully to take up the dangling reins. She glanced down upon Laura's wretched form. Tears flowed down Charley's face as she tied the reins around Mickey's saddle horn. Once she secured the stallion's reins, he seemed to settle down. I surmised that because the horse had been trained by a woman, that it took a woman to settle him.

I moved Chino forward into a fast trot to reach the women. I dismounted and moved to Laura, my eyes stung with sweaty tears as I fumbled in my pocket to produce my pocketknife. Charley slipped Laura's boot from the stirrup on her side. A moment later, Laura flopped into my arms like a wilted flower. I half dragged, half carried her out of the saddle.

I looked into Laura's ashen face, and more tears streamed down my cheeks. I turned to carry her to the creek side where I lay her gently in the soft grass. I leaned close to her chest to listen carefully for Laura's breathing. She seemed so weak and without response to the movement.

I called to Charley, "She's alive, but we have to hurry. Bring a canteen. She needs water."

I again leaned down and spoke to Laura, "Laura, open your eyes. It's Cole. It's Cole Stockton."

Charley moved to my side with the canteen and a strip of cloth that she had torn from her own shirttail. She poured water on the cloth, then used it to tenderly clean Laura's dirt streaked face. She then saturated the cloth with water, dabbing it generously on the dried bloody material of Laura's shirt, letting let it soak in.

The coolness of that water on her face caused Laura to open her eyes ever so slightly. She looked directly into my sweat-stained, unshaven face, and worry-weary eyes.

I brushed the dampened hair from her face as I mumbled something unintelligent like, "Can't leave you for even a little while without you going and getting yourself shot again." I swallowed hard to fight back the cracking of my voice. She closed her eyes again, floating back into dark unconsciousness. Charley brought a blanket roll from Mickey to place it around Laura.

"Check her wounds," I motioned to Charley. She eased Laura's soiled shirt and chemise up to reveal dried blood on her bruised and swollen side.

Charley looked up at me with a solemn face. "Make a fire to heat some water. I'll care for her. After that, go and roll yourself a smoke, or better yet, take a rest—you need it."

It suddenly struck me that I was dog tired. Even so, I bowed my head and closed my eyes for a moment. My prayers had been answered. Laura was alive.

Afterward, I scavenged up some dry wood to build a low fire. It occurred to me to see to the horses. I unsaddled all three, hobbled the black and let them all fend for themselves amongst the grass. Next, I moved to my saddlebags and produced the flask of whiskey that I carry for medicinal purposes. Right now, I could use a swig. Then, I passed the flask to Charley who smiled for the first time since our search found Laura. She, too, took a swig before using the whiskey to disinfect Laura's wounds.

Laura moved with a start as Charley seeped whisky on her wounds. She stared wide-eyed and fearful, yet unable to speak. She gazed up into Charley's deep brown eyes, seemingly to ask, "Who are you?"

Charley smiled down at her, whispering, "I'm his friend. Cole Stockton loves you very much, but won't come right out and say it. I guess most men are like that. Marshal Stockton is a good man. He saved my life, just as he hounded your horse's trail until we found you. You have lost some blood, but you should be all right, with a lot of rest, and care. No doubt, he will provide it."

Laura relaxed her feverish body, then lay back to allow Charley to care for her. Charley continued to speak softly to Laura as she cleaned her wounds.

* * *

Charley prepared Laura for travel, dressing her wounds, reassuring her with more woman talk. At dusk, I decided that we should wait until morning to move Laura back to the wrangler camp. Staying the night would give me time to rig up a makeshift travel bed. I figured she couldn't ride.

Using my sheath knife I cut two long poles and a few strong branches from saplings along the creek. Along with the remnants of Laura's rope I fashioned a travois.

That night, we made Laura a beef broth. I shaved jerky into a tin cup with water and heated it over the fire. Charley tore up the spare shirt from my duffle for bandages. My prisoner was quite the doc when it came to patching up a person.

It took a while, but I was able to spear a couple of trout with a long pole sharpened on one end. I broiled them on a forked stick over the fire. We had cool creek water as well. Fresh fish was our fare for the evening.

The next morning, I rigged the travois behind Mickey. Charley would ride him with Laura on the travois. Travel would be slow, however, Laura's resolve to live and Charley taking care to make her ride as comfortable as possible, we would make it. I would lead Laura's black stallion.

By early afternoon the wrangler's campsite came into view. Judd Ellison and the wranglers raised a cheer for us as we entered the makeshift camp. To tell the truth there wasn't a dry eye amongst Laura's men.

My burly prisoner was still alive and that set well with me. After seeing Laura's condition, her wranglers wanted to throw a rope around his neck and let a horse drag his hanged carcass all over the territory. I felt the same way deep in my heart, but I was an officer of the law and the law is what it would be. I would take him alive to answer for his foul deeds.

With Laura safely with us, the next problem loomed in my thoughts. Someone had to ride for wagons, a doctor, and Wyoming law. I couldn't do it for fear that some of that gang would return, trailing Charley and me. It would have to be Charley.

I called her to me, "Charley, I have another job for you. It's one day back to Fort Laramie and about three days on to Fort Russell. I am trusting you to mount up on Mickey in the morning and ride to Fort Laramie for a cavalry escort with wagons and the post surgeon. We will hold on here until you return."

Charley stared at me with a startled expression. "You mean," she stammered, "you are trusting me to ride away from here on my own and actually come back with help?"

"Yes, Charley, I am. I've watched you closely during our travel. I believe that you will help people in need, regardless of what awaits you in Denver."

She hung her head for a moment. Then, when she raised her face, she had the look of appreciation and determination. I knew that I could trust her with this challenge.

The next morning, Charley stood by while Judd Ellison saddled up Mickey. Judd eyed Laura's Winchester rifle in the scabbard and looked toward me. I nodded and he left it there.

When Charley turned to me, I handed her Laura's gun belt. "You might need this as well," I told her. I continued, "We'll look for you sometime tomorrow. Ride like you were with me—careful. Watch the skylines for movement. Check your back trail at times and always look for places to hide, should you need it. Good luck, Charley."

Charley put shoe to the stirrup and swung herself into the saddle. After situating herself in the saddle my special prisoner pulled her floppy hat down securely. She forced a smile for me. I nodded, then she turned Mickey and put slight heel to his flanks. They bounded into a steady lope northward toward Fort Laramie and our salvation.

With Charley on the way, I turned my attention to Laura and the wranglers. Water was running low which meant that I had to replenish. That was the easy part. I recalled a creek a few miles back. Judd gathered up the five empty canteens while I saddled up Chino. Leaving Laura was difficult, yet I was the best choice to go for the life-giving water. I mounted and moved out toward the east with that notion in mind.

* * *

Charley rode without incident for the first half day. At just past noon she traveled around a steep hill into a surprise encounter with a group of five rough men. Two drove a freight wagon, while the others herded livestock before them.

Something didn't set right with the bunch, and Charley sensed trouble. She sat Mickey to watch as they approached. Something told her to shift the revolver at her side to a more comfortable position, and she did.

The wagon slowed to a halt before the young woman. She watched the men's eyes. They burned bright with lust. One on the wagon gazed with a crooked grin, his glare pierced her body.

Then, he spoke, "Well, Missy. You look like you traveled a bit. You must be worn out and need some food. We can make camp right here. Come join us for a bite and a drink."

"No, thanks, I'm not that tired," replied Charley, her right hand set at the butt of Laura's Colt Lightning. The man noticed right away that her jaw was set and the position of her hand to the weapon. He nodded and waved her away, still grinning with greed for her.

Charley turned Mickey to pass the burly men when two who were herding stock leaped their mounts at Mickey. Charley instinctively laid her hand on the butt of the Colt, cocking it in the same motion.

Her response surprised even Charley. She fired twice. The first bullet grazed one man's cheek. He whipped his right hand up to feel the wetness of blood oozing down his cheek. The next round burned the second man's thigh, bringing a wince of pain. They immediately backed off, but attacked her character with a stream of profanity.

"Don't come any closer," Charley called out with steadfast determination. As a second thought, Charley motioned with the revolver, "And, don't try and follow me. It would be the last thing you want to do."

Revolver in hand, Charley put heel to Mickey and off they went at a fast gallop. Her mind raced as the young woman relived the incident. "I think they were scavengers and that they stole that wagon and stock. What if one of them had pulled a gun? What would I have done?" She recalled the confrontation once more. Then, thoughts turned back to Cole's advice, "Watch your back trail every now and then." Fortunately, the men did not follow her.

When she was a couple of miles away from the rowdies, Charley pulled Mickey to a halt and dismounted. She leaned against the black horse, her heart still pounding wildly. "Oh, Lord!" she breathed aloud. "I must be more careful." Within a quarter of an hour she was once again astride Mickey. This time she watched the landscape with infinitely more care.

Just past the last shadows of dusk, the sentry called out, "Halt! Who goes there? Identify yourself!"

"I'm Charlene Westbrook and we need help bad!" She wearily blurted out to the young soldier.

"Sergeant of the Guard, post number one!" resounded the soldier. Within minutes, Charley found herself surrounded by a sergeant and four troopers who escorted her to the Officer Of The Day.

* * *

The day turned bleak for those of us at the wrangler camp. A stout Wyoming wind rose and howled for an hour or so, bringing dust and insects that clogged our eyes and nostrils. We covered our faces with bandanas and pulled hat brims down low over our eyes.

Judd coaxed the animals to lie down, then he covered their heads with saddle blankets in an effort to keep them free of infestation.

A quick rain shower followed the strong wind, turning the prairie into mud. The flame went out and our campfire lay smoldering. Judd attempted to restart it with damp tinder. He eventually found some dry wood and brought the fire back up. Those men who could move about searched out more fuel to keep the flames fed.

By early evening the cavalry detachment, ambulances, and the post doctor came upon us. Charley rode in the lead with the officer in charge, a lieutenant. The doctor quickly set about checking each of the wounded before dressing their wounds. He took Laura first, deeming her situation more serious than the rest.

Charley visited with Laura while I explained the situation to Lieutenant Hodges. He expressed sympathy for our plight. In the morning, he would escort Laura, her wranglers, and my rustler back to Fort Laramie for additional doctoring and the guardhouse.

I sat with Laura until she drifted off to sleep. She looked a whole lot better than when Charley and I found her. With her wounds tended to and knowing that her wranglers and I were with her had rekindled her spirit. Why, she even smiled at me at bit. I leaned down to kiss her forehead, whispering, "My dearest Laura, I'm always with you in thought. I'll stay beside you though the night. My love is with you always."

The Army detachment bedded down in our makeshift camp. Come daybreak, the troopers loaded the wounded into the ambulance wagons. A detail of two troopers took charge of my prisoner for safekeeping to the Fort Laramie guardhouse. After all, he and his friends had rustled government consigned horses. Surely, the Army would eventually turn him over to civilian authorities for trial.

I bid farewell to Laura and her wranglers, advising that I would come to the fort within a week to escort them home. Laura seemed alright with that. Presently, she needed medication and rest from her ordeal and Fort Laramie had the closest hospital. I knew the soldiers would take good care of her and her boys.

Charley and I stood on the open prairie next to Chino, Mickey, Laura's new black horse, and our trusty packhorse as we watched the cavalcade of soldiers and wagons move out of sight toward Fort Laramie.

"Well, Charley," I said, "let's you and I go see Judge Wilkerson."

She started to take off Laura's gunbelt and I stopped her. "Keep it a while longer. We still have some wild country before us, and I might need some help." Charley managed an appreciative smile before turning, mounting Mickey, and taking up the black's lead rope.

CHAPTER NINE

Charley and the Judge

Charley and I watched the cavalry detachment escorting Army ambulances with Laura and her wranglers fade from view. Then, we climbed into the saddle. She rode Mickey and led Laura's prize stallion. I took charge of our trusty pack animal as we turned southward toward Cheyenne.

I outlined my plans to her as we rode. "Charley, the plan is to return this packer to Fort Russell and board out Chino, Mickey and the black with the cavalry stables. We will take the train to Denver."

Charley looked at me wide-eyed, "Marshal Stockton, I ain't never been on a train before. I've seen them and they fill me with fear. I mean, there was all that huffing and puffing—and I've seen fiery sparks fly from that smoke stack. I feared that it would start a raging prairie fire that no one could put out. I just don't know about such things."

I chuckled under my breath and thought, "Young lady, you are in for an adventure."

As miles faded behind us, my charge opened up a bit more—asking questions about the big city of Cheyenne, what the train ride would be like, and she even talked a bit about her childhood. She mentioned that she was the eldest daughter of a Kansas farmer. Her parents needed seed money, so when this Westbrook feller, her deceased husband, took a notion to her, they embraced the marriage so long as he would provide a reasonable dowry to them. I guessed that a lot of young girls got away from their families like that.

Anyway, she told about how Westbrook hankered for greener pastures than Kansas farmland and decided to move them to the Colorado Territory. When his crops failed, he turned to liquor for courage and cards for luck to win a big pot to restart their life. The Devil's brew got the better of him.

Later that evening, over hot coffee and another tin plate of beans, salt pork, and biscuits, Charley looked like she had something gnawing at her. I studied her a while before asking, "Something bothering you?"

She lowered her eyes for a moment, then responded, "Yes. I thought all day long. What's that Judge like? I mean—is he a fair man? Would he send me to prison somewhere instead of hanging me?"

I answered her the only way I knew how, "Judge Wilkerson is a fair man." In the back of my mind, I also wondered just what he would do in this case. Once again, I related my stand in the matter, "As for myself, I uphold the law. I don't make the judgments, but I'm sure that the Judge will be fair with you." She nodded without speaking, but with worry in her eyes.

When the fire burned down to embers, we rolled up in our blankets. I closed my eyes trying for sleep; however, my mind churned with all sorts of thoughts of Charley's situation. She had proven herself trustworthy to me, but she still had to answer to His Honor for the shooting.

I tried to put myself in her shoes. The only conclusion that came to me was that I would have shot the SOB myself. Well, I had pretty well decided by this time, that when we arrived in Denver, I would speak on her behalf. Could I make a difference in the outcome? Just then, a peaceful feeling came over me. I drifted off thinking about Laura—how it must be a miracle of the Lord that she was spared.

* * *

On the trail about a day from Cheyenne, we came across a line of four heavy wagons angling toward us from the west. Giving our mounts a breather, I studied the wagons. Actually, there were two freight wagons, each with a six mule team and double hitched to a second wagon. Each wagon was piled high with hides.

This outfit appeared to be a group of buffalo hunters. I thought about that. Perhaps they might stop for a mid-day meal and if neighborly, we might be in for a change of menu. Beans and biscuits get a bit old after several weeks on the trail.

We let the wagons get a bit closer before heeling our horses forward to meet with them. The four hunters turned out to be a bit trail worn and uneasy talking to us. Still, they showed manners toward the lady.

They quickly pulled off hats and exchanged pleasant greetings, "Howdy, Ma'am." When one noticed the star on my shirtfront, he yelled out, "Howdy, Marshal. We had a good hunt and now on our way to Cheyenne to bargain our bounty. We were looking for a noon-day stop for coffee and a bite to eat. Would you join us for some roasted buffalo?"

Now, that was the offer I had hoped to hear. "Buffalo is hard to turn down," I replied.

The hunters halted their wagons, unhitched the teams, and within minutes, had strung out a picket line for their animals. A bewhiskered Jake Saunders fancied himself a singer and entertained us with ballads while gray-haired Jeremy Platt built a small fire, then dragged out a spit. Their younger men, Tad Bernard and Sid Taylor, tended the stock with buckets of water from barrels on the lead wagon. They even watered our animals for us.

When the fire was going good, Jeremy brought out bit of hump roast and ran the spit pin through it. Within a half hour, Jake put his knife to carving thick slices of buffalo meat. I could see that Charley enjoyed the fare as well as the men enjoyed having as they put it, "a pretty lady" as their guest.

When we had eaten our fill, Jeremy thought to put a thick slice of that roast into a square of cloth that he fashioned by cutting a flour sack down to size. "Here's a bit of meat for the road, Missy. It goes good, sliced thin on a biscuit."

Charley smiled at him and the feller turned a bit goofy. "Shucks, we got lots. You are welcome to it."

Back on the trail, my companion announced, "That's the first buffalo I've ever eaten. I liked it a lot."

Early the next afternoon we arrived at Fort Russell where I arranged for our three animals to board in the cavalry stables until I returned the following week to pick them up. The Army took back their packhorse and the mount that I'd borrowed to escort Charley Westbrook back from Canada.

Captain Lloyd, the Post Adjutant, welcomed me back and arranged for an army ambulance to take us to the Cheyenne train depot. The corporal who drove the wagon got us there in plenty of time to board the afternoon train to Denver.

With thirty minutes to spare, Charley and I sat on a bench on the depot platform while I rolled myself a smoke. The magnitude of the train awed her. After several minutes, she turned to me, "Marshal, are we O.K. to ride this train?"

I was taken back by her question, "Why, yes, Charley, we are. What made you ask that?"

"Well, Marshal Stockton, everybody that is here waiting for the train seems kind of dressed up. We are looking like we just came from farm chores—and no doubt we smell like it."

I looked around and got the very same feelings. For the first time since arriving at the depot, I studied the people around us and sensed their *holier than thou* stares at us.

I turned and took stock of Charley's appearance—dusty Levi's, shirt with a torn sleeve, scuffed shoes, stringy hair, and floppy hat. I looked down at myself. My trousers and sweat-stained shirt looked like I'd slept in them for quite some time, and I had.

I tried to remember the last time that either of us had taken the time to bathe. I laughed out loud as I replied to her, "You know, Charley, you are absolutely right. We look like a couple of rag muffins."

I stood to survey the crowd waiting for the train. Then, I grinned. At the far end of the depot platform were a couple of cowhands as well as some gents who looked like buffalo hunters to me. No doubt they would be riding in the last train car. I decided that we should join them.

I motioned to my charge, then grabbed up my Winchester rifle and saddlebags. Charley stood with her blanket roll in hand. I took her arm like a gentleman and escorted her to the far end of the platform. As we walked arm in arm, I smiled and extended a greeting with a tip of my hat to all the ladies we passed.

Charley began to giggle a bit and by the time we got to the last rail car, we were both giggling. No one on that platform could possibly have dreamed of the wild adventure we had on our way to Cheyenne.

When it was time to board the caboose, where the train brakemen and conductor rode, the rough-looking men we chose to ride with stood aside and allowed Charley to board first. They were courteous, tipping their hats with a grin. I caught no looks out of bounds. We made ourselves comfortable on the straight back wooden benches that serve as seats. The engine whistle blew, and with a burst of steam, a hard rock back, and lunge forward, the train began the journey to Denver.

I surmised that we would arrive around suppertime. A plan came to me about how to get Charley all gussied up in order to meet the Judge. She must be dressed appropriately and I just knew that my boarding house partner in crime, namely Ma Sterling, would love to assist.

The cowboys sipped from a single bottle of whiskey and swapped stories as the train rumbled and clacked down the tracks. The hunters also had their jug with them, and spoke in low tones about their best hunts. I caught the men every so often stealing looks at Charley. I could tell that they thought her quite attractive in spite of her trail-worn clothes.

My young companion spent most of the trip looking out the window of the rail car, marveling at the speed we were traveling and taking in the landscape. Suddenly, she turned to me with the realization, "Marshal, we're awful close to Denver. I recognize that mountain shape."

I peered out the window and agreed, "Yes, we should arrive within about half an hour."

I spoke just as the conductor James Wilson stopped behind me with his railroad watch in hand. Wilson had been the conductor on a couple of my previous rail trips. He corrected me with slight smugness in his voice, "We shall arrive in exactly twenty-one minutes and my time is never off."

I hated to admit it, but the Cheyenne to Denver train arrived at the depot at exactly the time predicted by Wilson. I stole a glance to see him laughing. I nodded my apologies for doubting his accuracy.

Once the train came to a complete stop, we rose to leave the car and step down to the depot platform. The cowboys and hunters seemed a bit tipsy, but stood to full height, and with appreciative nods, beckoned Charley to step down first. I followed her, intent on moving in front to help her down to the platform. There was no need to.

When Charley reached the bottom step of the caboose, Denver rail porter Moses Jordan was there with a step stool. He reached up to take her arm and help her down to the platform. She smiled at him saying, "Thank you." Moses whipped off his porter's hat and bowed somewhat, "You welcome, Missy."

Then, he looked up at me, "Welcome home, Mista Stockton. I hope yo journey was good."

I replied, "Thank you, Moses. It was a very interesting trip. By the way, how is Miss Etta?" Etta was his wife.

He smiled a bit and related, "Etta is a fine woman, Mista Stockton. You know that she like you a lot. She ask me all the time if I seen Marshal Stockton."

I knew from previous conversations that Etta was feeling poorly. I reached to my right hand trouser pocket and found a twenty-five cent piece for the elderly man. Moses stared at it for a long moment before looking up at me. Guarded emotion seemed to be there, "Thank yah, Suh, Mista Stockton. You are a good man."

Charley and I walked to the front of the Denver depot and looked up and down the street. Her eyes opened wide with wonder. "I ain't never been to Denver City. It's so big!" she exclaimed.

I admitted that it was a large town. I looked at her squarely and asked, "Would you like to walk the streets some?"

Her eyes lit up with a sparkle, "Why, yes, I would. Thank you, Marshal. It may be the last time I get to see a big city." I sensed the sorrow in her voice.

I pointed out places of interest as we walked down the street. Without thinking, I pointed out the courthouse and jail. Charley turned to start toward the jail. I stood there a moment regretting what I'd done before calling out to her, "Charley, where are you going?"

She looked back at me saying, "To jail, Marshal. That's why you traveled all that way to fetch me back here. I need to answer for the killing."

I took a deep breath and replied, "Charley—let's walk a bit further. There's a friend I want you to meet."

With a puzzled look on her face, she shrugged a bit but sided me again. A few blocks later, we turned toward a residential district. She had a questioning look on her face.

"It's all right, Charley. We'll see the judge tomorrow morning. In the meantime, we need to clean up a bit, get some proper food, and a good night's rest."

Soon, we arrived at my home away from home in Denver. We entered Ma Sterling's boarding house parlor. I could see that supper was on the table and it sure smelled good. Boarders gathered around the table, chit-chatting as they enjoyed Ma's fried chicken and biscuits.

I rang the bell, not wanting to just walk on in with my special guest. Momentarily, Ma Sterling was with us, looking surprised to see me. She looked at Charley with calculating eyes. "Cole! Why are you standing out here? You are one of my regulars. You should have come straight on in. Who is your friend?"

"Ma Sterling, I want you to meet Charley," I hesitated a moment, then corrected myself. "I want you to meet Charlene." Well, Charley looked up at me, and Ma Sterling caught the surprise on her face. I continued, "Charlene has to meet with Judge Wilkerson in the morning and this is all she has to wear. I figure you know how to help her."

In her wisdom, Ma Sterling knew exactly what I meant. Charlene was my ward for something serious. "I understand, Cole. I know what you need of me. Well, let me tell you this. I know you Marshals very well, and before Charlene meets with the judge—she will have a bath, hair fixed properly, and a nice dress. I don't suppose that you Marshals understand that, but a young woman needs to look her best when in public. Now, instead of parading your friend through the scrutiny of the dining room crowd, you take her through the hallway to the kitchen. I'll meet you there to take care of everything. You just leave it to me, Mister Stockton. I'll take good care of your friend."

As Ma Sterling suggested, I ushered Charley through the hallway to the kitchen avoiding the boarders in the dining room. Ma entered the kitchen a few minutes later and sat Charley at her small table in the corner.

"Now then, Charlene, before we draw a bath, I do hope you like fried chicken with all the fixings," uttered Ma, as she went about filling plates for the two of them. Seeing the obvious pleasure on Charley's face, Ma Sterling continued, "When we're finished with this, there's a thick berry cobbler for dessert."

I could see that Ma Sterling had taken charge of Charley's welfare. I excused myself to leave the boarding house, and walk the mile to Judge Wilkerson's home. When I knocked on the door, Marie

Wilkerson, the judge's wife answered. "Marshal Stockton! What a surprise. Joshua is in his study. I'll announce you."

I stepped inside the Judge's home. Because of my dusty trail duds, I waited in the foyer. Marie returned to me within minutes. "He will see you now, Marshal."

I followed Marie to the door of the study. She smiled at me, then turned and left me to open the door and enter. I took a long breath, momentarily closing my eyes in an attempt to picture what I was going to say to this man who upheld the law along with me. After a hard exhale, I knocked once. "Come in!" came the response.

I opened the door and stepped into his study, which looked more like a library to me. Judge Wilkerson sat behind his large wooden desk. His spectacles sat low on his nose. He raised his eyebrows, "Marshal Stockton! Have you my special prisoner in your ward?"

"Yes, Sir, I do," I replied.

The Judge questioned further, "And, is she in my jail?"

I shook my head to the negative, relating, "She is safe enough for now."

The Judge nodded while he moved from his desk to a sideboard across the room. He opened a door and produced a bottle of whiskey along with two glasses. "I presume that you want to discuss the matter. Let's savor a bit of my fine Kentucky vintage while we converse."

That set well with me. I have to say that his whiskey was good. I let him start the conversation. "Now, what say you about my special prisoner, Marshal Stockton?"

"Judge Wilkerson, I tell you here and now that this woman acted in self defense and the killing of Frank Westbrook was justified." The wise elderly man eyed me close as he asked, "Would you, Marshal Stockton, swear to that in a court of law?"

"I will, Judge!" I blurted out, and continued with the story that Charley related to me about the killing, as well as her journey to Canada. I then spoke of our journey back to Denver, including that the three brothers of her deceased husband had set out to kill her.

Wilkerson listened intently as I affirmed my trust in Charley, including the trust I placed in her when I gave her a weapon to defend herself, and for her ride for help to Fort Laramie.

I continued, "Charley Westbrook followed my instructions each time we met with trouble. She worked tirelessly to care for wounded wranglers, and gave her undivided attention to the extensive care of Laura Sumner. She did all this as only a person who cares about people's welfare could."

I concluded with the statement, "And, she came back here quite voluntarily to answer to you for her alleged crime." The judge caught that word *alleged* in my tone.

We sipped on whiskey in silence as the judge thought through the circumstances and a course of action. Finally, he looked at me with somewhat of a knowing grin and firmly advised me to have the special prisoner in his office at ten o'clock sharp.

"She'll be in your chambers at the appointed time," I acknowledged to Judge Wilkerson. I let myself out. I needed a bath and shave. Then, I would see if Ma Sterling had set out some of that fried chicken and biscuits. She had.

* * *

At precisely ten o'clock the next morning, Charlene Westbrook and I stood at Henry's administrative desk just outside Judge Wilkerson's office. Charley whispered to me, "I'm a bit uncomfortable in these clothes, Marshal. I've never had anything as fine as this."

I assured her that it was all right. "You look very nice. In fact, I'm like you, I'm not used to wearing fancy clothes either," I said. Charley lowered her eyes a bit, a slight blush on her cheeks.

Charlene Westbrook stood smartly dressed in the deep purple suit and ivory blouse that Ellen Sterling loaned her. A simple broach lay at her neck. Her hair was combed into a bun. Henry appeared quite taken with her appearance.

Myself? I had dressed in the aging suit that I kept for court appearances. I did sport a decent white shirt and black string tie. We were ushered into the judge's chambers forthwith.

To my surprise, there were others in the judge's chambers as well, including the territorial prosecutor. My eyes spanned the room quickly to also see the county sheriff, a known gambler from the Four Aces saloon, two town constables, two women who were employed as saloon girls, and one Deputy U.S. Marshal—my friend, George Jamison. Henry took his place as recorder.

I escorted Charley to a large chair before His Honor and stood next to her. She looked up questioningly into my eyes. I knew nothing about the presence of this room full of people. The fear on her face made me believe that my companion for the last several days thought that she was about to be sentenced to hang. I reached down and took her right hand, giving it a quick reassuring squeeze.

What transpired next was the strangest court proceeding that I'd ever participated in. The Judge turned to Territorial Prosecutor, Tyrell Hewett, and asked him to address the specifications of his warrant.

Hewett stood tall and in a courtly manner related, "The charge is the shotgun murder of Frank Westbrook. I requested a murder warrant against his wife, Charley Westbrook."

The Judge inquired, "Do you have anything to add Mister Prosecutor?" to which Hewett replied, "No your Honor, I do not."

Judge Wilkerson then turned to me. I was dumbfounded. "Mister Stockton, as your charge's attorney, how do you plead this case?"

I stepped forward to stand in front of Judge Wilkerson and stated, "Charlene Westbrook is innocent. I escorted her from Canada to Denver. During that trip, she related to me the sequence of events that led to her husband's demise. I believe her story and she pleads not guilty." I returned to stand beside her.

Judge Wilkerson turned to Charley and said in an authoritative voice, "Do you wish to receive justice within this proceeding, or do you wish a full court trial with a jury of your peers?"

Charley tugged at my shirt sleeve, "What does that mean?"

I leaned toward Charley and answered, "The Judge is asking whether you want to continue here in his office, or do you demand a full court with a jury of twelve men to judge you?" I emphasized the words *twelve men.*

As I anticipated, Charley whispered to me, "I will do this proceeding."

I stood to face first of all, Tyrell Hewett, and grinned at him. Next, I addressed Judge Wilkerson. "Your Honor, my client accepts this proceeding as fair judgment."

At that moment, the judge turned to Hewett and asked a critical question. "Do you, Mr. Hewett, after being apprised of the circumstances, still want to pursue a murder trial?"

Prosecutor Hewett looked uneasy as he surveyed the people in the judge's chambers. He in turn asked Judge Wilkerson as to who the people other than the law officers were and what was their relation to the case. Judge Wilkerson in all his wisdom related that the persons assembled in his chambers were merely witnesses for the court.

Hewett seemed unnerved. He again took stock of the court's witnesses before announcing, "The Territory of Colorado retracts all charges against the person known as Charlene Westbrook, alias Charley Westbrook, in the murder case of Frank Westbrook. It is hereby determined that the defendant acted in self defense of her life."

Judge Wilkerson quickly addressed the court clerk, "Henry, write out a copy of Mr. Hewett's statement. He will sign it before he leaves this room."

Then, the Judge addressed the prosecutor. "Mr. Hewett, please approach the bench."

Prosecutor Hewett went to stand before Judge Wilkerson. I could not swear to their quick conversation, but I think I caught something to the effect that Hewett remarked, "Joshua, you old codger, you got me this time." To which, I thought I heard the Judge tell him, "Tyrell, between us two old codgers, I believe that justice is surely served." Again, I wouldn't swear to it, but I thought that they shook hands before Tyrell Hewett moved back to his chair to gather up his notes.

Judge Wilkerson turned to Charley and said, "The defendant will rise and face the court." Charley eased up slowly then stood straight. When I took her hand, she squeezed mine. I detected the shiver that ran through her body.

Judge Wilkerson announced to the gallery of people before him. "Charlene Westbrook, you have been vindicated of any and all charges concerning the demise of Frank Westbrook. You are free to go as you will."

Charley faced His Honor and asked with quivering voice, "Judge, I'm not too book learned. I'm not sure of what you just said. What did you mean when you said vindicated?"

Judge Wilkerson smiled at Charley, "Dear Lady. You are not guilty of any crime. You are free to live as you will."

Complete relief came over Charley's face. Overwhelmed, she had to sit for a few minutes. I stood there holding her shaking hand as she whispered over and over to herself, "I don't believe it. There is justice in this world."

The Judge watched in silence as Hewett signed his statement. Somewhere in the background, Henry announced, "All rise!" Judge Wilkerson disappeared through a private door. While people filtered out of the Judge's chambers, I glanced around the room.

To my surprise, I chanced to catch a quick intimate look that passed between Hewett and Mary Belle Jones, one of the saloon girls summoned for the Judge's proceedings as they exited the room.

It dawned on me then, that justice is served in many ways, not always with a badge and a gun, or a hanging.

Henry approached us then, "Please come back about four o'clock this afternoon. I will have the official documents announcing the court decision with Miss Westbrook's copy. I will also send the retraction of any wanted posters for her."

Charley rose from the chair to face me. "It's over Charley. You're free. Where would you like to go?" With watery eyes, Charlene looked up into my face and replied, "I would like to go to San Antonio. I've never been there, but I've heard that a woman can meet good men in Texas who need a woman to stand with them."

Thinking back to my own family and Texas roots, I agreed with her.

I took her arm, suggesting, "Let's get some lunch, Charley. It will be hours before we can get the court documents." Charlene Westbrook and I walked out of the courthouse to the nearest café. Charley's eyes misted as she recalled her arrest and our trip from Canada back to Denver. We ate in silence, but I could see that she had a lot on her mind.

That afternoon, we picked up the legal documents from Henry. Afterward, I took Charley back to visit with Ma Sterling and the opportunity for her a good night's rest.

The next morning, I escorted Charlene Westbrook to the Denver stagecoach depot where I saw her off to her next life's adventure. Several passengers gathered around the depot waiting to board the coach. A well-dressed young man took interest in Charley and was bold enough to ask her name and destination.

Charley smiled at him demurely while answering, "I'm Charlene Harwick. I'm bound for Texas and a new life." The young man beamed with excitement. "Let me introduce myself, I'm Jordan Bethany. I have a small ranch west of San Antonio. I would be delighted if you let me tell you about Texas as we travel."

Judging by the shy looks that passed between them, I figured that Charley was on her way to a better life. Before she stepped into the coach, however, she turned and threw her arms around my neck. She hugged with all her might and kissed my cheek.

When she released the embrace, she whispered to me, "Thank you, Marshal Stockton. You saved my life." The only thing I can say is that Charlene Westbrook was an amazing woman. The last I saw of her happened when she waved farewell from the window of the stagecoach.

Now, my thoughts turned to Laura Sumner. She and her wranglers were up in Wyoming at Fort Laramie. I meant to head back up there and see that they got back to her ranch without further harm. I would leave on the train to Cheyenne the very next day.

Chapter Ten

A Man to Reckon With

Early morning found me in Ma Sterling's dining room sipping coffee and partaking of a Ma Sterling special breakfast. Ma took leave of the kitchen long enough to visit a spell. She watched me for a few minutes while sipping her own coffee. Then, she commented, "I see that you are dressed for the trails again. It looks like the Judge is keeping you busy."

I looked up at her with a grin, announcing, "This trip is for me. I left a good friend up at Fort Laramie. I intend to bring the lady and her hired hands back to Colorado safely."

Ma tilted her head a bit pondering my statement before replying, "Your friend must be very special to you. If you get the chance, please bring your friend by for a visit." She held my eyes for a moment before adding, "You take care in your travels, Mr. Stockton." With that, Ma Sterling turned and entered the kitchen to finish preparing breakfast for the rest of her boarders.

Half an hour later, I stood on the Denver railroad depot platform with my saddlebags, duffle, and Winchester rifle in hand. With some time to spare, I thought to telegraph Captain Lloyd at Fort Russell. I requested him to have Chino and Mickey saddled and waiting for me at the Cheyenne depot. I thought that seeing Mickey would help Laura's spirits. Her black stallion could stay at Fort Russell. We would pick him up on our return trip.

Once again, I boarded the train to Cheyenne, finding a comfortable seat along the rear wall of the car. As is my custom, I scrutinized my fellow travelers.

My first interest centered upon a young man who appeared quite nervous. After the train chugged out of the station and gathered speed, I could tell that this young feller was up to something. Close to ten miles out of Denver, I glanced out the window and found another young man leading a horse. I thought to myself, "We are about to be robbed by an amateur." I slid the Colt out of my holster and waited.

A moment later, the youngster leaped straight up, drawing a handgun from beneath his coat. He yelled out, "This is a robbery. Have your valuables ready for my bag!"

Gasps of disbelief ushered from amongst the score of passengers. A few ladies uttered shrieks of fear and cowered in their seats. The would-be robber was excited by their response.

I cocked the hammer back on my Colt and waited for him to come to me. Suddenly, the man sitting behind the kid eased up and drawing his own revolver, swung the barrel of it to the young man's head. He instantly fell to the floor. Well, so much for an amateur robbery.

The train picked up speed and the rider with the extra horse in tow fell behind to wonder what happened to his companion.

I chuckled a bit to myself as the man who downed the would-be thief opened the lapel of his coat to proudly display a gold colored badge that gave notice of his job. He announced himself as a railroad detective, "Fear not fellow travelers. I am here for your protection."

I felt no need to identify with the situation and so slid my revolver back into the holster. I leaned back against the seat, pulled my Stetson down a bit and took a short nap.

Later, I sensed the slowing of the steam engine, wakening to the hard reverse of the large wheels that brought a jolt to the car. We had arrived in Cheyenne.

I waited until all the other passengers had vacated the car, including the railroad detective with his prisoner in tow. Breathing a sigh of relief to be closer to my destination, I grabbed up my possessions and stepped down onto the depot platform.

I found, much to my surprise, Sergeant Hoffmeister and Corporal Finnegan waiting for me at the depot. We shook hands around as Hoffmeister greeted me, "Good afternoon, Marshal Stockton. The captain told us that you would be coming on this train. We brought your animals saddled and ready as you requested."

After thanking the two soldiers for their kindness, I greeted Chino and Mickey. Both were glad to see me, muzzling my shoulders as I stroked their heads and necks. Both sensed that we were traveling.

After securing my duffle on Mickey, I turned to Chino. I slid my rifle into the scabbard and secured saddlebags and bedroll behind the saddle cantle. I was ready. Putting boot to stirrup, I swung into the saddle to take up Mickey's lead rope and then led north out of Cheyenne at a walk.

Once out of the city and on the rolling prairie, I allowed the horses to break into an easy lope. I wanted to get as close to Fort Laramie as possible before we camped for the night.

Near twilight I crossed Horse Creek and made my camp. After unsaddling both horses, I let them graze freely. I knew that neither would go far. I build a low fire to brew myself a bit of coffee in a tin cup. That coffee and a piece of jerky was my fare for the night as I traveled light for this mission, bringing only ground coffee, jerky, and biscuits.

By dark, the sky filled with twinkling stars providing my only light. I listened for the telltale sounds of nature, assuring that all was well. There was the slight splash of fish in the creek along with the unmistakable croaking of frogs. I rolled up in my blankets, then slipped off into thoughts of Laura. Over a week had passed since we found her and by now, she should be well enough to travel.

* * *

At daybreak, I woke up with another tin cup of coffee and a fire-warmed biscuit. For some unknown reason to me, I mentally recounted the wrangler story of how the rustlers came upon them without warning. With that recollection, a foreboding shudder traveled through my body.

The point where Laura and her herd were attacked would come up sometime that afternoon. I wondered then if that rustler gang would prey upon a single rider with a spare mount just as they had with a full trail drive. I would have to watch carefully for sign.

The morning passed peacefully. In the early afternoon I became wary of my surroundings. Was someone watching me? Carefully, I scanned the horizon, but didn't detect anything out of the ordinary. Still, the uneasy feeling clouded my mind. My senses sharpened as I looked and listened for those familiar sounds of the prairie—barking prairie dogs, rasping grasshoppers, and bird melodies. I heard none. The absence of these voices of nature meant imminent danger.

Out of nowhere they came, about a dozen riders approaching fast on my back trail. I figured them for what they were—the remainder of the rustler gang. I sunk spur to Chino. We three stretched out in a dead run. Mickey, being rider-less, kept pace along with Chino.

The sharp crack of rifles sounded behind me as well as the whistle of flying lead as it sailed past us. Suddenly, Chino faltered, then broke stride. I chanced a quick look down to find the big roan hit hard. Blood flowed profusely from his stomach. I quickly looked forward to see the rising knoll close ahead. "Come on, Chino—the hill!" I yelled, pointing him toward it.

My faithful companion put forth his last valiant effort to reach the crest. Once there, I quickly dismounted, drawing my Winchester, before stepping clear as Chino faltered for the final time. This brave animal screamed in pain and crumbled to his knees. Tears of rage and grief filled my eyes as I drew my Colt and shot him in the brain, ending his suffering.

I got Mickey over the crest of the hill behind Chino, then coached him to lay on his side as Laura had taught him. With Mickey's reins wrapped around my left wrist, I steadied my rifle across the top of Chino, and lined up on one of the rustlers. Just as soon as the rifle bucked against my cheek and shoulder, I levered another round into the chamber to fire at another target. Both men slumped backward off their mounts.

Now, it looked to be about ten men against one—the odds shifting more to my liking. I grinned hard against the sadness in my heart. They wanted me dead, and they were going to play hell doing it.

Images flashed through my mind of this ruthless gang. I thought of the vicious, lusty glances on the faces of those who attacked Charley and me—of the brutal, murderous attack on Laura's horse herd, and of the savage quickness with which they had just now come up on me.

They would pay for it. They would pay dearly with their lives. I would see to it. That these men would try to circle me was without question. Once done, they planned to rifle me full of lead. Bill Hickok's words of wisdom filtered into my mind, "When outnumbered, make every shot count."

My adversaries dismounted, then spread out. Their rifles went to work spraying hot lead toward me with ten guns, and I fairly had to keep my head down. Spurts of dirt spit high into the air as round after round burrowed into the earth around me. Bullets whistled through the air and I heard sickening splats as bullet after bullet tore into Chino's body. My loyal horse protected me one last time. My one advantage was that I held the top of the knoll and could watch their movements below.

I hunkered close to the ground and peered down at them. Two men chanced moving in opposite directions to flank me. I slid my Winchester along Chino's neck and led the man working his way toward the right of me. Fire increased from the front as a ruse. I waited as he worked his way along the ground. He finally made the mistake I waited for. He raised into a crouch and at the third step, my bullet caught him in the upper body. He went down hard, throwing up his arms, and never moved.

I immediately rolled the opposite direction to catch the man running to my left with a quick shot that burned his hind end. He went down screaming in pain. All went quiet. I figured they had begun talking amongst themselves.

I chuckled bitterly to myself. I was not the rube they took me for. They faced a seasoned gunfighter and they were about to receive an education. Their numbers were no match for quick thinking and an accurate shot.

An hour ticked by, yet they lay still waiting for me to make a mistake. At this point, I knew that the first to make a wrong move was the first to die. I calculated that they were waiting for darkness. They would work their way a lot closer with no light to give away their movements. Well, that wouldn't come for a couple of hours. I'd be waiting for them.

In the meantime, I fumbled around to find my canteen, then wet my neckerchief, and put it against Mickey's muzzle. He was a smart horse. Mickey lay there just like I wanted him to. He would be my last hope for an even break. "Rest easy, Mickey," I told him in a whisper. "We might have a hard ride ahead of us."

Another hour passed with no gunfire. That gave me the thought to liven things up a bit. I scanned the prairie as sweat stung my eyes, looking for color that didn't belong there. "O.K.," I thought, "sometimes, you just got to shoot, whether you hit something or not."

I squeezed off and got no response. Twice more I fired into that colorless mass and got no response. A second later a good deal of lead ploughed up the earth all around me. I grinned hard and let out a stream of unrepeatable phrases. "Well, they aren't napping anymore," I thought.

As quickly as the response came, it ended. At least they knew I was alive and willing to deal with them. From the direction of the sun, I figured about an hour before sundown. Then, the real challenge would come. I expected some would try to snake belly up on me. It could become a nasty situation.

While I had time, I worked fervently on dragging my saddlebags out from under Chino's carcass. Luckily, the earth was somewhat soft. After several painstaking minutes, the bags came free. The underside of my bags held the extra ammunition that I desperately needed. Breaking open the boxes, I replenished the cartridges in my belt, and ensured the loads in each of my two revolvers. I also fully loaded the Winchester.

I chanced a look over Chino's neck to find that those boys had moved back about twenty-five yards and had a fire started. I could almost taste the coffee and roasting meat. My stomach let me know then that it was past suppertime. I took a swig from my canteen, imagining it as hot coffee.

It occurred to me that I'd hit some of them in their previous positions. Even though they had moved back some, maybe I could still reach them with my rifle. I thought, "Maybe I'm crazy, but Kentucky windage might come in handy here. No matter, I need to keep them stirred up."

I lined up the Winchester straight to my target, then squeezed off a round. It fell short about a dozen feet, but did cause a scramble amongst them. I nodded to myself before raising the muzzle a bit. I squeezed off another round. The bullet smacked into a saddle. They moved back a few more feet, filling the air with the din of loud cursing.

Now for some serious shooting. I raised the muzzle a bit higher, lining up on a dark figure. I squeezed off and watched as the silhouette raised slightly before slamming straight backward. Return fire immediately rang out, but their lead fell some three feet short of Chino. Well now, that gave them something to ponder.

Myself? I felt the odds definitely swinging in my favor. The rustlers' fire died down mighty quick after that.

"Got to get ready now," I mused. "Those guys are going to be coming in soon to rush me."

I waited without motion or sound for them while removing a piece of tough trail jerky from my shirt pocket. Something about chewing on cold jerky irked me. I guess because any other respectable man would be at home with a loving wife, sitting at a nicely prepared table. His supper would be hot. Perhaps he would be having a big beefsteak with lots of good coffee. More often than not, I was stuck in some miserable situation staring death straight in the eyes.

I was tired, I was cold, and I was getting more angry by the minute. My mind seemed to play tricks on me as I thought, "I wish those guys would just come right on up here, so I could shoot hell out of them."

Yet another thought hit me then, "The hell with this. I'm going down there and kill as many as I can before they get me."

I eased down the back slope and got Mickey to his feet. Then, I swung quickly into the saddle, shoving my rifle into the boot. This skirmish was going to be revolver work—close in and deadly. I figured that surprise truly was on my side.

I turned Mickey down slope over the backside of the hill, hesitating only a moment. Then, I turned him again, heading straight for Chino's body. We jumped over my beloved horse, and rode in a galloping charge smack dab at the center of the gang.

A dark shadow raised quickly in front of me. I shot him in the face. Another loomed up knife in hand. Again, my shot was deadly. Because the others heard the shots, they knew I was coming. They now scrambled all over. Most became easy pickings since my charge caught them in a relaxed state, never imagining that one man under siege would turn the tables to barrel right into their camp.

One man rushed me from behind. I swung Mickey in a hard turn causing the horse to kick out at him. The feller fell backward into the hot coals of their fire. He thrust up screaming, his clothes on fire. The poor devil lunged onto the prairie and rolled from side to side still screaming in anguish.

The entire melee lasted some ten minutes. Mickey and I had ridden full gallop right down on them. Our surprise attack had caught them off guard.

As quickly as we rode in on them, we vanished back into the darkness to our knoll. Once again, I moved into the defender role to wait. How many I'd killed or wounded, I wasn't sure, but I knew that the tide had turned.

The remainder of the night resounded with cries for help from the wounded. Once their campfire burned out, those able saddled up their mounts and made a dash for safety. I dare say that it could not have been more than three or four that rode off into the night, leaving their companions where they lay.

The first light of day brought a grisly scene. A lone man lay hunkered down behind a downed roan horse with a black horse behind him. Four outlaws lay in the throes of death. Another three lay mortally wounded, including the burned one. With the usual loyalty of thieves, and murderers, the remaining members of the rustling gang had disappeared into the night.

An hour after dawn, a twelve-man cavalry patrol rode upon the scene out of the north. First Sergeant Angus MacTavish halted his Fort Laramie patrol to take in the bloody scene, "Damn," he cried out loudly. "It looks like a massacre."

The soldiers saw movement from the knoll and waited with weapons drawn. Momentarily, a lone figure on a black horse trotted down slope to meet them. The man looked weary, sweat stained clothes clinging to his body. He wore the silver star of Deputy U.S. Marshal on his shirt. Sergeant MacTavish motioned his men to put away their arms as he greeted the lawman.

Daylight came, yet I stayed at the top of the knoll waiting for movement below. None came until I observed an army patrol moving warily onto the scene. I eased up to my feet and got Mickey upright, then I mounted to ride quickly down the slope to meet the patrol.

"I'm First Sergeant Angus MacTavish commanding a patrol from Fort Laramie," The leader announced. "Who might you be?"

I replied with authority in my voice, "I'm Cole Stockton. I'm a federal officer and I had an unfortunate encounter here."

The sergeant looked around hardly believing what he saw. "Lord Almighty, how'd you do it?" he questioned. Troopers gathered around to hear my reply.

In somber tone, I related the events of the evening passed saying, "I just plain got mad at being bushwhacked." I continued, "Sergeant MacTavish, I am running late on a very important mission. Would you have your men bury the dead and arrest the wounded? They are all rustlers and murderers. Please bring the living to Fort Laramie with you." I turned and looked sadly toward the knoll where Chino lay. "Please bury my horse up there and bring my saddle and trappings to Fort Laramie with you. He was a good friend."

Being a veteran cavalryman, the sergeant understood what I meant. "Aye, Marshal. We will take care of everything. Will you be at Laramie when we return?"

"That I will, Sergeant," I replied as I mounted Mickey to ride away toward Fort Laramie.

Sergeant MacTavish turned to the troopers crowded around him. He pointed to Cole Stockton in the distance, uttering, "Aye! Laddies, look around you. There rides a man to reckon with. All right now. We've work to do before returning to the fort."

* * *

Just over a week had passed since Laura Sumner and her wranglers arrived at Fort Laramie for medical help. She was quartered on the second floor of the Post Hospital. Today, she was up and about, although still stiff and sore. She was never the less able to navigate on her own.

Laura rested in a chair next to the window of her upstairs hospital room. She thought of Cole Stockton. Where was he? He had left with that young woman Charley, the one who dressed her wounds so tenderly. Laura thought back to the rustler raid. All of their stock was gone. Some of her men had been killed. All this because she couldn't wait for Cole Stockton to return to her ranch to help with the drive.

Yet, what difference could one man make in that situation? What difference could one man make against so many?

Laura felt weak and vulnerable. She leaned against the window sill as the tears continued to stream down her face. Suddenly, a familiar whinny filtered through her sobs, and she raised her face to peer searchingly out the window.

Riding toward the hospital was a ragged slender man on a black horse—Mickey. Laura couldn't stop the tears. Now, they became tears of joy, and they flowed even more freely.

Laura watched Cole as he wearily dismounted, then tied Mickey to the hitching post. He looked exhausted. In fact, he half stumbled as he stepped upon the plank porch.

The ranch woman made her way to the door of her room, which set slightly ajar. She listened intently for a moment, then returned to the chair out of breath. Momentarily, Laura heard muffled words exchanged downstairs.

Then came the sound of boots on the steps, spurs jingling. She breathlessly watched the door to her room. It opened slowly, and there stood a haggard Cole Stockton, holding his weather-beaten Stetson in his hand.

Cole remained at the door a moment, looking into her blue eyes. Then, he stepped forward. She struggled to rise, bringing him immediately to her side. He took her hands, gently pulling her to her feet. Her arms slid around his sweaty neck, and his arms around her, holding her as tightly as he dared because of her wounds.

Laura nuzzled against his weather-beaten, whiskered face, then gazed up into his eyes. Embracing, no words passed between them, yet each heart spoke to the other, "I love you."

Chapter Eleven

Taylor Thornton

The following day, Surgeon Captain Moore confirmed that Laura and her men were fit for travel. I arranged with the post adjutant, Captain Lloyd, for an army ambulance and a six trooper escort to Fort D.A. Russell at Cheyenne.

Arriving at Fort Russell three days later, I visited the cavalry stables to retrieve the black stallion that I had boarded there. At the Cheyenne railroad depot, I arranged space for Mickey and the black stallion in the stock car to Denver. With rail transport arranged for the horses I then made my way to the window for tickets for Laura, her boys and me.

From Cheyenne, we took the railroad to Denver where Laura purchased a wagon for herself and her wranglers. I rode Mickey beside the wagon with Laura's prize black stallion in tow. We followed the stagecoach road toward Miller's Station.

When we arrived at the ranch, Laura's trio of wranglers left behind gave up their chores to jubilantly gather around us. Scotty helped Laura down from the wagon and hugged her gingerly, then kissed her on the cheek. He exclaimed, "Laura, we read about the rustler attack in the paper. My God, it's good to see you all alive."

Eli Johnson shook hands with the returning trail hands, then acknowledged the new men as he spoke about working the ranch with them. Afterward he stood in line for his Laura hug.

Mike Wilkes, the rather shy youngest hand, shook hands with the returning men before standing demurely in front of Laura with hat in hand. She smiled at him for a moment, then grabbed the boy and gave him a firm hug, finishing with a kiss to his cheek. I would swear that Mike's face turned the color of a blush rose.

That evening, the ranch family held a memorial for the fallen. We partook of roasted venison, compliments of the home trio. In their spare time while Laura and the wranglers were on the drive, the men built a stone pit to barbecue whatever meat or game was on hand.

The next day, Laura went back to business. Her integrity with her boys reinforced their respect for her as she used the money that the Army paid for the Fort Russell horses to pay them for the trail drive. She offered jobs to Jeff Sutton, the colored trail hand, as well as Jim Borden. Both men accepted her offer. Sutton seemed to be the most grateful. Still, the fact was that the rustlers evidently made quick sale of the stolen animals. That herd was never found.

Within even the most dire circumstances, sometimes a silver lining appears. First Sergeant MacTavish and his troopers investigated thoroughly while burying the dead outlaws, to include searching the deceased for identification. His report to Wyoming civil authorities resulted in a just reward made out to me for destroying the menacing rustler gang. Laura needed money to keep her ranch going so I turned it over to her.

The fact remained that I was horseless and needed a good mount. Chino had been my horse, my friend, and constant companion for several years. He knew me well, and did what I expected. He had a sixth sense about him. It grieved me to fire the shot that relieved his misery, knowing he gave his all when needed.

Laura offered the black stallion that she was so proud of, but I just could not take him. He was Laura's horse—her prize. After much thought, she named him *Sultan*. Sultan would insure quality breeding from which to build a more solid horse ranch foundation. She figured that she could take the offspring to train a lot easier than wrangling the wild out of captured horses. Just having him sort of made up for the loss of her herd to rustlers. Yes, I agreed. Sultan should become the mainstay of the ranch's herd.

Laura's boys rode hard, searching every trail, pass, and mustang hiding place. They found a good many more wild stock, and I was offered my choice of them. Somehow, none of them suited my taste, nor my needs.

Since I was in between assignments from Judge Wilkerson it was a perfect time to hang around the ranch. She loaned me a fine roping mount, Brandy, an amber-colored mare. She was solid and quick. Yet, Brandy was a ranch work horse, and not a mount that I could trust on the wild trails I rode. I thought long and hard about where my next horse would come from.

We had been back to the ranch about a week when a single rider came up the trail late in the day. He led a packer along with another dark colored horse. I recognized the rider as he turned into the ranch yard. Taylor Thornton was a rancher from down in the New Mexico Territory. I stepped to the bottom step of the porch to greet him, "Taylor. What brings you up Colorado way?"

"Well, Cole," he replied, "I heard tell through the grapevine that you were in need of a horse. I got this one—he's from my personal string and a good one to boot. I'll bet that he'll fill the bill for what you want in a horse. You know that I owe you. So, I figured the least I could do was find a worthy mount for you. He's among the best I've ever seen."

"Let's look him over," I suggested, stepping off the porch. Taylor was right beside me. The animal was a magnificent, dark chestnut with lighter mane and tail. He had a blazed face with one white half stocking on his right rear fetlock. He stood proud and solid. I liked the looks of this stallion. When I spoke softly to him, he nuzzled my shoulder, and seemed to say, "Take me, I'm yours."

Taylor suggested that I saddle up and try him out. I grabbed mane and swung myself up on his back. He felt good under me, so I rode him over to the stables to get my gear. The chestnut responded well and seemed anxious to go for a gallop.

I found the horse well trained, standing trail hitched while I outfitted him with blanket and saddle. Then, I put boot to stirrup and swung deftly into the saddle. We started out at a quick walk. Once past Laura's ranch gates, I touched heel to his flanks and we were off like the wind. He definitely liked to run and his gait stayed smooth.

Quickly, we began getting acquainted with each other. I liked the feel of his strong muscles and sensed his intelligence. Now, I needed to find out one other thing. I slid out my Colt and quickly fired three rounds in rapid succession. The horse never flinched. It was as if he had anticipated gunfire. He met the final challenge.

We boiled back into Laura's ranch yard like the Devil was on our tail. At just the right point, I sawed back on the reins, and the stallion slid to a stop. He was definitely the mount that I needed. I smiled as I dismounted. Finally, I had found my next horse.

Turning to my old friend, I inquired, "What do I call him?"

Taylor grinned widely as he announced, "I call him Warrior. He seems to have that spirit about him."

It took me only a moment. Looking into the animal's eyes, I declared, "Warrior it is then." I patted his long sleek neck. He appeared to enjoy it.

I glanced up to the porch. Laura stood there smiling, nodding her head—"Yes." She followed with, "Taylor, come join us for supper."

"I'd like that," replied Thornton, and he followed Laura into the house while I took Warrior to the stables and found an appropriate stall for him. I laid out a handful of grain along with the hay that I pitched in his feed box. I filled the water bucket before I took a few minutes to talk with him.

* * *

Laura had an innate ability to put a man at ease with her conversation over a meal. She filled us each a plate of roasted beef, oven baked potatoes, fresh green beans, and fresh baked bread. Later, she topped it off with a large slab of homemade berry pie. The coffee was freshly ground and steaming hot. I wondered, "Could a man ask any more than this?"

Taylor answered my question without knowing it. He grinned a bit, then asked, "Cole, when are you two going to get hitched? A man needs to leave a legacy for future generations to ponder. I'd surely like to be there when you do. I'd help make it the shindig of the century. Why, folks would come from miles around—just to see the bride, of course."

I glanced over at Laura. I'd seen that sparkle in her eyes before. It happened while we danced at the *Spring Fling* in town. I held her tightly as we danced those slow ballads. She looked stunningly beautiful to me that day. Her smile and expressive eyes stole my heart. That memory stuck with me, providing some comfort when out on the trails of the wild Colorado. This evening, it sort of came full circle.

"Maybe," I thought, "it is time for something more than to be figured as a close partner." I would have to think hard on this. I had often uttered before that I didn't want a woman to wonder, if, when I rode off, I might not come back—alive.

My mind churned with more thoughts of Laura as I considered, "True enough, I like being around her. The times that we are in each other in our arms and kiss—w-e-l-l, she is quite a woman. We have grown on each other. We understand each other in a way that speaks of a closeness to be cherished."

My senses returned to reality when Laura spoke up, "In due time, Taylor—in due time. We're still trying to figure out if we like each other enough."

I looked at Laura at that moment to find that same sparkle shining brightly within her crystal blue eyes. She in turn looked directly at me and she smiled.

Taylor immediately countered with, "Shucks, Laura. Everyone sees it but you two. Like just now, when I mentioned ya'll hitching up. Cole looked at you, and you looked at him. I could feel the heat of a raging prairie fire between you two."

"Taylor!" exclaimed Laura as the blush rose in her cheeks.

"Oh, all right. I'll leave it be—for the moment," retorted Taylor, and he continued, "But, mark my words—the day will come, and I sure want to be there when it does."

Laura folded her arms in front of her and gave Taylor a mock scowl. Taylor laughed out loud, "Well, I do know what I'm talking about."

Laura smiled then as she turned to me, "Cole, let's go into town tomorrow. There's some supplies we need. That is, if you still wish to eat at this table."

I swallowed before responding. I had gotten used to Laura's good home-cooked meals, so I readily agreed. "I'll even drive the ranch wagon."

Laura, Taylor, and I spent the remainder of the evening with coffee and friendly conversation. Near midnight we finally bid our good nights, and I showed Taylor to a spot in the bunkhouse.

Chapter Twelve

The Hawk

They called him *The Hawk*. At six foot three, his imposing muscular frame caused even the most hardened man to shudder. His eyes were black as a raven, cold as steel, and piercing. He seemed to stare right through his victims, unnerving them at the split second of decision. His hooked nose was reminiscent of a hawk's beak. A jagged knife scar adorned his left cheek and he often bragged of the fate of the man who put it there.

Hawk wore his dark brown hair long to his shoulders in the fashion of most plainsmen and frontier scouts. He wore a low crowned hat with straight brim pulled low to shield his eyes.

Hawk always wore dark colored shirts under a tanned hide vest that carried an intricately beaded hawk on the back, along with a smaller one on each panel of the front. The symbol of his nickname—*The Hawk*. There could be no mistaking him with others.

Nothing was too lavish for Hawk's image. He wore his bone handled Colt .44 low on his right hip in an ornately tooled holster. His cartridge belt was beset with silver Conchos and turquoise stones. His highly polished black boots jingled with each step as large-roweled silver Mexican spurs spun round and round.

Presently, he sat his buckskin horse in the Colorado wilds watching two riders approach slowly on the trail in front of him. Both men wore suits and ties. They looked like money—rancher money.

Hawk was a hired killer, and it was evident that these men wanted someone dead, someone important. Yes, they wanted someone dead—someone too fast and too good for them to handle. Others before had come to Hawk knowing that he was the best. His price was steep. These men knew his reputation. They knew that Hawk was their man for this job.

Hawk loved his work. He was fast, he was vicious, and he liked being the talk of the town where he visited. He knew his name struck fear in those he vanquished. His reputation as one of the fastest guns alive gave him immense satisfaction. His usual way meant goading a man into drawing against him—a deadly mistake.

The two rich strangers faced him now as he scowled his contempt for them. They had money. He would do their chore even though he had no respect for them. They were cowards in his eyes. Hawk grinned wickedly as he looked both men straight into their eyes. He asked point blank, "Who do you want me to kill?"

Much to his delight, the two men averted their eyes from his stare, pausing with lowered eyes. One finally disclosed their need of him. "There's a federal marshal who is standing in the way of some big dealings. We want to bring in our own lawman." The rancher swallowed hard before continuing with strained voice, "We want you to get rid of Cole Stockton."

Hawk grinned slyly. While he had never met Stockton, he knew the man's reputation with a gun. This job could be his greatest victory. He would be the man to claim he gunned down Cole Stockton. Hawk took great pleasure thinking of how his reputation as a gunfighter would surpass what folks thought today. He would be most famous.

Hawk had contemplated Stockton before, but had been preoccupied with earning large sums of money. Now, the time seemed right. Yes, he would take their money, but only as a token—this one he considered gratis—free of charge. Stockton's reputation nagged at his mind, and the more he thought about it, the more it appealed to him. He would study this man, Cole Stockton, find his weakness, and when the time was right, he would goad him into making that one fatal mistake, like so many others before him—drawing against the Hawk. Hawk smiled at the prospect. He planned to enjoy this.

* * *

Hawk arrived in Miller's Station near midnight the next evening. Once his buckskin was stabled at the local livery, he made for the hotel, and secured a room. He was adamant about the room facing Main Street and his scowling face frightened the night clerk enough not to argue. This room would provide an opportunity to observe all activity in this small town. Hawk fell asleep dreaming about the forthcoming challenge. In his mind's eye, he was already the victor. He would let the entire West know about it.

Around ten o'clock the following morning Hawk seated himself in one of the chairs along the hotel boardwalk. He rolled a smoke, lit it and began to size up the town as folks went about their business. Hawk spotted Sheriff Lawson immediately. Lawson was a young man with a smile for everyone he encountered. Hawk studied the young sheriff for a long moment and thought, "Young and inexperienced for this sort of work. I'd bet he's fairly fast with that revolver, but more likely to want to talk his way out of a fight than use it."

A ranch wagon driving up the street caught his attention. The young woman on the seat was quite attractive. She had long dark hair and shining blue eyes. Hawk reflected to himself, "I'd sure like to get to know her better." But, for now, business came before pleasure.

The man holding the reins of the team, however, was a bit older. He appeared tall and lanky with sandy hair. Something seemed familiar about him to Hawk. The man's face seemed stoic. His eyes took in everything in a glance as he drove the wagon team. Yes, that was it! That was not the face, nor were they the eyes of a rancher. Hawk contemplated the man. His manner indicated someone who had faced the beast. This man was a—gunfighter.

Hawk watched carefully as the wagon pulled up in front of the general store. He observed closely as the driver jumped down from the wagon and walked around to help the woman from the wagon. He noticed the revolver strapped low around the man's waist and the position of the walnut-gripped pistol butt in relation to the man's hand, always at wrist level.

Hawk observed his walk. It was the walk of confidence. The man stood out as someone who was ready for trouble at the drop of a hat. This man would be a challenge.

Hawk turned as the door of the hotel opened and the clerk stepped out to light up a smoke. He looked to the clerk and asked casually, "Who are the folks in front of the general store?"

"Why, that's Miss Laura Sumner, and Marshal Stockton. They are real close. Some say that they'll marry soon. Isn't she a beautiful woman?" The clerk waited for a response, but Hawk was already moving across the street toward the general store.

Hawk needed to study this man Stockton up close—to size him up. Hawk entered the general store, pretending to browse at the guns and ammunition counter. He carefully watched Cole Stockton as he followed Laura Sumner throughout the store, carrying the shopping basket in his left hand—his gun hand free, always.

Laura sensed a disturbing presence as she gathered her purchases. She glanced back to meet the eyes of a man in black. The dark piercing gaze upon her shot a forbidding shudder through her body. It felt as if the Devil himself had her in his grip.

Cole Stockton sensed something distracting Laura as well. He too looked around to meet with Hawk's piercing study of Laura. The two men held their gaze directly into each other's eyes, and each man saw death staring him in the face. It was Hawk who turned away first, only to walk slowly out the door of the general store.

For the first time in his life, Hawk felt sweat beads forming on his forehead. The palms of his hands were sweaty. No man had ever caused him to feel this way before, and it bothered him greatly. In past encounters, he had always made the other man uncomfortable. There was something in Stockton's eyes that told a dark tale of swift and deadly action when the chips were down. A shiver ran through Hawk's body, as if he had somehow seen his own body laying crumpled in the dusty street.

This man, Stockton, would take more observation in order to get the best of him. He would not be goaded like the others. Stockton was more than an experienced gunfighter. He had values. He could only goad Stockton because of something that meant a great deal to him. That woman, Laura Sumner—she was the key.

*   *   *

Cole Stockton remained extremely quiet as he and Laura drove back to the ranch. Laura also had something on her mind. She turned to Cole suddenly and spoke of the man in the general store. "Cole. That man in the general store made me feel very uncomfortable. I noticed that he and you stared at each other for an extremely long time. Do you know him?"

Cole waited a moment before replying. "No, Laura, I don't know him, but I know of him. He is known as The Hawk. He is a hired killer. At the moment, I don't know if he is wanted for anything. As such, I couldn't take any action with him. I do suspect that he is here in Colorado on some business. It would be deadly business. I sense future trouble with him. I may have to face him, and word has it that there is none better than The Hawk."

Laura thought quietly. She knew what was on Cole's mind, "Can you take him, Cole?"

"I don't know, Laura. I just don't know, but I'll be careful. Don't worry about it."

Laura knew better. Hawk was on Cole's mind and nothing that she could say or do would ease it for him. In these situations, Cole would have to work it out for himself. Laura knew also that Cole's job was one of those things that kept them from a closer relationship. In her mind, Laura wrestled with the knowledge that, as long as Cole lived, there would always be somebody wanting a reputation as a fast gun. There would always be someone coming who thought himself faster and better than Cole. That bothered her.

That Cole wore a badge justified his actions in defending himself. Judge Wilkerson knew it, Laura knew it, and Cole knew it. At least he could use his gun for the law and not against or around it.

* * *

Later that afternoon, Hawk became extremely edgy. He had stared into the eyes of Cole Stockton and knew that his challenge would be met. He had to choose the right time, a time when Stockton would be caught off balance. A twinge of doubt entered into Hawk's mind.

He had to find someone to goad into a gunfight to reassure himself. The sheriff, yes, Sheriff Lawson would suit him perfectly. Lawson was young, fairly quick, and possibly a friend of Stockton to boot.

To kill Sheriff Lawson in a standup gunfight would set Stockton to worrying. He would do it within the week. He would show Stockton just how fast that he, The Hawk was.

A few days passed before Laura Sumner rode into town to pick up a few more items from the general store. She saddled up Mickey and trotted into town alone this time, but armed with her Colt Lightning revolver.

Laura arrived at Miller's Station to a deserted street. She wondered why as she rode warily down Main Street. In front of the livery stables she observed two men facing each other across a distance of ten yards. Laura recognized the two men immediately. It was Larry Lawson, the Sheriff, who was facing Hawk. Each man reached for his gun as one.

Sheriff Lawson's gun had not cleared his holster when the Hawk shot him not once, but three times in the center of his body. Lawson was dead before his body touched the ground. Hawk stood grinning as he casually opened the loading gate of his revolver, punched out empties and reloaded three fresh cartridges. He still had the touch.

Laura rode up at a gallop with the shots, jumped from Mickey, and bent down over Sheriff Lawson. She was there before the townspeople crept out from behind closed doors.

Hawk saw his chance and grabbed the dark haired woman by the arm. He disarmed her growling, "You're just what I need. You're my good luck charm, until your man, Stockton, comes to me. Then, we'll see about you and me being together."

Hawk pulled her into the livery stable and closed the doors. He threw Laura down into the first stall. "Stay there," he commanded. Then, he sat down at the entrance of the stall—his eyes taking in all of her beauty. Laura felt ravaged by his eyes.

"Cole Stockton will kill you," she stated coldly to Hawk's face.

"I'm counting on that he will try," replied Hawk. "I was sent here to kill him, and now he is going to come to me. You can watch me kill him." And then, Hawk grinned at Laura with lust burning brightly in his eyes.

Chapter Thirteen

Split Second Decision

One of the best ways for man and horse to bond is to take a sunrise ride. My thought was exactly that. Rising in the still of pre-dawn, a cup of hot coffee wakened my senses to the task at hand. Warrior stood ready in his stall and I felt eager to test the stamina of my new mount.

Warrior was definitely both spirited and intelligent. As I entered the stables, he immediately recognized me and moved forward to greet me with enthusiasm. He appeared ready for a good run and that was what I happened to have in mind.

After saddling up, I led him out of the stables to find Judd Ellison who greeted me with a smiling face, "Cole, I think you got yourself a damn good horse. What you going to do this morning?"

"Judd," I replied, "we're going out for a considerable ride. Probably be back early afternoon. Tell Laura that we're on the trail of understanding," I chuckled a bit. "Both you and she know that one."

Judd nodded as I mounted and turned toward the western side of Laura's LS Ranch, intent on riding the wilds of the Rocky Mountain foothills to a special place.

I worked Warrior through various calculated movements and gaits. The horse did so well the first hour, we paused for a rest. Still, the chestnut stallion seemed anxious for more. My position as an officer of the law demanded a worthy mount, one that responded to my every movement. Sometimes a Marshal had to rely solely on his mount to carry him through unknown territory. He relied upon his horse to alert him to danger, to help find water sources, and to be his salvation in dire times. Those qualities framed this day.

Three hours into the ride, we reached the place I had in mind. I stripped the chestnut of all riding gear and turned him loose. Would he stay with me, I wondered? It was a long walk back to Laura's ranch if he didn't.

The stallion looked at me as if to say "You are crazy." Free of halter and saddle, he seemed a bit hesitant at first, then moved toward me. I stroked his face and neck, speaking softly to him before turning my back on him. I closed my eyes.

In a moment, his warm muzzle laid on my shoulder. I laughed lightly. This horse likes me. Turning to face him, again, I stroked his long neck for a few minutes before turning toward the stream where clear water babbled over rocks at one end to form a deep pool along the shoreline at the center. I dropped to my knees, bent forward, and drank of the cool water. A minute later, the muzzle of my new partner dipped into the life-giving liquid to drink as well.

Water dripping down the back of my neck startled me. I shivered a bit and turned around to come face to face with Warrior as he tested me. Well, I had it to do. I eased up to full stance and told him what a good horse he was.

A thought of earlier years came to mind and once again I was a young man. I stripped off my gunbelt, laying it close to the shoreline. My hat, boots, and clothes followed. Then, naked as a jaybird, I jumped into the water and frolicked as a silly kid. Warrior grazed lazily nearby, but never left my sight.

* * *

Warrior and I returned to the LS Ranch mid afternoon to find Judd Ellison with worried eyes. Unlike his usual coolness, he appeared highly distraught. "Cole!" he cried out while wiping watery eyes. "Laura is in peril."

Bending down from the saddle to hear his words more clearly, Judd blurted out the story of Sheriff Lawson's demise at the hands of Hawk. Judd trembled as he fought to clear his voice. "Cole, Hawk has Laura in the livery stable in town. He's issued a challenge to you, making it clear that he came here to kill you. He also made clear his intentions toward Laura afterward. I don't need to tell you what he intends."

My mind flashed back to Hawk in the general store, our eyes jousting for leverage, correctly surmising his intended target. Anger flooded my mind and body. My first inclination was to ride off immediately into town to face him. I would go into town and kill this man known as The Hawk.

Stern faced and silent, I turned Warrior away from Judd and galloped to the ranch house, dismounted, and once inside, sought out my second Colt revolver. I loaded all six chambers with instant death and remounted Warrior. Out the gate we went at a gallop, turning onto the stagecoach road to Miller's Station.

Visions of Hawk filled my mind as we covered the miles into town. My blood boiled as I thought of this man—this hired gun, who sought to end my life and defile my beloved. I hated him. I hated those like him. Memories of past gun fights rushed through my mind.

Hawk embodied a vicious man who lived to instill terror in the hearts of ordinary people. I would end his viciousness. Vengeance sprang into my mind and wrought my soul with abandon. The thought blazed across my mind, "To hell with the law. This is personal."

A rake of spurs urged Warrior to stretch out at a run as we ate up the distance to Miller's Station. Upon entering, the town looked deserted. Town folk hid in fear as they watched and waited to see which of us would prevail—which of us would lay dead and bleeding in the street. I shuddered, but clenched my teeth.

I turned Warrior to the hitching post in front of the Star Light Saloon. After securing Warrior to the hitch, I turned and strode up Main Street towards the livery. My eyes searched each building I passed. Caution heightened my mind. Every step taken brought visions of those who faced me in times past. Breathing came easier now, my mind clearing for the task at hand. Bill Hickok told me time and time again that a man wrought with anger is a dead man.

I stopped and closed my eyes for a moment before the last block of buildings, exhaling a long breath. Hesitating briefly, I stepped into view of the livery, my right hand slightly touching the butt of my Colt. A blanket of calmness seemed to envelope me as I called out, "Hawk!—Hawk! You wanted me. Here I am! Come out and face me!" I didn't have to wait long.

One door of the livery swung wide open. A moment later, Laura stood in the doorway. She was disheveled and distraught but otherwise in control of herself. Hawk came behind Laura holding her right arm tightly up behind her back. He pushed her roughly out in front of him, taking a few more steps toward me. His gun remained in his holster as he sneered at me. His eyes, however, told the story. He planned to use Laura as a shield while he drew and shot me.

Laura squirmed around, trying her best to offer me a clear shot at Hawk. Yet this strong man held her right where he wanted her. "Well, well. Here is the infamous Cole Stockton. Guess what Stockton! Your woman is a real beauty, and we're gonna get to know each other a lot better after I kill you."

I watched his eyes, setting myself to take lead, steeling my mind against the inevitable pain that was coming. Reality returned as I continued to look into his eyes for that instant telltale flicker. The wait—always the wait. The palm of my gun hand itched. It wouldn't be long now.

Hawk's eyes glinted for an instant. His lower lip twitched slightly. His right hand flashed for the gun at his belt. My own hand immediately filled with the butt of my Colt. Laura screamed. The report of Hawk's revolver filled the air, as the intense burn seared into my upper chest.

I grunted with pain, staggering back, and as I did so, Hawk threw Laura hard to the ground, his revolver rising and lining up for another shot. My Colt thundered and bucked in my hand, once—twice, and as I slumped to the ground, blinding pain and darkness swirled all around me. I prayed that I had taken The Hawk with me.

* * *

Laura, in Hawk's clutches felt the slight flinch of his body just before his hand flashed for the bone-handled Colt at his holster. Her eyes immediately went to Cole Stockton. His hand moved. A flash of the wrist, and the Colt rose smoothly out of his holster—his thumb cocking the hammer back in one fluid movement, leveling. Hawk's revolver reverberated as the muzzle spewed fire and hot lead. Powder smoke filled the air.

Laura screamed as she was thrown roughly to the ground, her breath momentarily knocked out of her. She gasped, fighting frantically for air. She looked up to see Cole stagger backward.

Hawk's expression was one of disbelief. Stockton had beaten his draw, but had not fired at him. No matter, he had shot the Marshal. Now he was going to finish the job. Hawk stepped forward, cocking his revolver again.

Without warning, the realization of what he had just done flashed across his mind. He had thrown the woman down, and now he stood vulnerable. He stared at Stockton. The man was still on his feet, and the deadly bore of his Colt was staring right at him. Stockton's weapon suddenly belched fire and hot lead.

Hawk felt the searing pain as the .44 slug took him straight in the chest. He staggered, desperately trying to raise his pistol to line up on the lawman again. A second bullet hit him close to the first, causing his finger to spasm as he pulled the trigger. The shot fired into the ground.

Hawk looked down at the stain spreading on his shirtfront. Next, his eyes saw the ground rising up to meet him. Hawk hit the ground hard, his eyes glazed, his mind in a fog. Cole Stockton had beaten his draw. In a split-second decision he elected to take the bullet, rather than risk hitting Laura Sumner, and waited in pain for his chance. Hawk exhaled his last breath and passed on to the court of a Higher Power.

Cole crumpled to the ground, face down in the dirt. His hand still held the smoking revolver, cocked for the third time.

"No!" screamed Laura, as she scrambled to his side. She removed the Colt from his limp hand, eased the hammer down, and slipped it behind her belt. Townspeople emerged from their hiding places, and rushed to the scene. They gathered around Laura and the fallen men.

Laura looked up with a tear streaked face pleading, "Get a doctor! Someone get a doctor! He's been shot. Oh, God! Cole's been shot." Laura leaned closely over Cole's face and cried out, "Dammit, Cole Stockton! Don't you die on me. You can't die on me. I won't let you."

Suddenly, strong hands pulled Laura away from Cole. She fought them as four men crouched around his limp body. Picking him up carefully, they carried Cole to the closest building—the restaurant.

Laura pushed through the crowd to walk directly behind them. She shouted "Take it easy with him! He's hurt badly."

Curious onlookers crowded around Hawk's lifeless form. An old timer with white beard looked down at The Hawk and mumbled, "He don't look so tough now." Another man nodded in agreement.

The four citizens rushed Cole Stockton into the dining area. Others hurriedly cleared two tables and shoved them together. A waitress rushed clean table linens to the scene, quickly spreading them over the makeshift operating table just before the men laid Cole gently on his back. "Where's that doctor?" shouted one man just as Doctor Simmons dropped his bag in front of the table. He leaned over Cole and immediately began tearing open his shirt.

Laura stared at the unconscious Cole. Her eyes riveted on his chest drenched in blood. His face was ashen. His eyes remained closed and his arms lay limp at his side. He was oblivious to touch or pain.

Doc Simmons's resolute face revealed his concern as he blotted the blood to examine the wound. Sweat beads broke out over his forehead. He looked up at Laura who hadn't made any move to leave. "Get her the hell out of here!" he yelled, then turned his attention to the grim detail of probing for the bullet.

One of the men who helped carry Cole to the restaurant took Laura by the arm to escort her outside. She resisted at first, then realized that she could do no good at Cole's side. Concerned acquaintances who had crowded around the restaurant entrance moved aside as Laura and the gentleman left the establishment.

Laura's knees went weak, nearly crumbling to the plank boardwalk. The man led her to a wooden bench nearby. She sat with her head in her hands, waiting for word from Doctor Simmons.

Momentarily, Laura sensed a presence. She looked up to see Miss Donahue, the proprietress of Marlene's Millinery who smiled at her, offering a hanky. The woman motioned silently for permission to sit beside her. Laura acknowledged allowing Marlene to join her on the bench. The curious citizens of Miller's Station had crowded back at the windows of the restaurant, each jockeying for a view of the doctor laboring over Cole Stockton.

Laura gratefully accepted the hanky, wiping tears and dust from her face. Without a word, Marlene reached into her handbag to produce a monogrammed silver flask and offered it to Laura.

Laura nodded, then discretely took a sip of the amber liquid. She closed her eyes as she swallowed the spirits. She handed the flask back to Marlene who took a quick sip as well before returning the flask to her handbag. The two women clasped hands as they awaited news of Cole's condition.

Somewhere in the background, Laura heard a man lament, "Damn it all—did you see it? Marshal Stockton just stood there and took that bullet. Then he shot The Hawk to doll rags."

* * *

Doc Simmons probed fervently over Cole Stockton to locate the bullet lodged several inches into his upper chest. "God," he breathed, "Three inches lower and I wouldn't have to dig for this bullet."

A long four hours later, Doc Simmons stepped out into the cool evening air. Most of the curious had departed for their homes or to the saloons to talk about the day's excitement.

He looked down at the tear stained, haggard face of Laura Sumner, took a deep breath, then spoke, "I got the bullet. He was hit very hard, and is in a state of shock. Only time will tell now. You can see him, but for only a minute or two. I don't want to move him for a few hours yet."

Simmons stopped to swallow and clear his throat before continuing, "Laura, I did my best, but I don't know if it is good enough."

Laura forced a weak smile, rose slowly and quietly entered the restaurant. An exhausted waitress sat quietly at Cole's side. She had assisted Doctor Simmons with his procedure and now watched over the patient. The restaurant reeked of carbolic acid.

Laura walked quickly to Cole's side touching his arm ever so slightly. He was ghostly pale, lying helpless on the makeshift operating table. The waitress excused herself for some fresh air.

Laura stood gazing at Cole's haggard face before her eyes moved to his hands. They were not the rough hands of a wrangler, but those accustomed to skilled work. She reached down to take his right hand in hers. It felt cold and clammy, not the warm hands that she cherished. The memory of their first meeting flashed vividly across her mind.

She leaned close to his face. His breathing was shallow, but he was alive. Laura brushed back his sweaty, tangled hair then kissed his forehead tenderly. She whispered into his ear, "Cole, it's Laura. Don't leave me. I love you very much."

After several long minutes, she rose, turned and wiped the fresh tears from her eyes. A low, hoarse whisper momentarily startled her, "Love—You—too." Laura turned quickly back to Cole and caught a glimpse of a flicker of his swollen eyelids.

She returned to him. That was the sign. She knew that he would live. Cole had already drifted off into a world of restless slumber. Laura whispered to him, "Rest now, my love. I'll be right here by your side. Rest now, and get well."

A few curious passersby peeked through the restaurant's windows. Doctor Simmons and Taylor Thornton returned to Cole's bedside. Taylor studied the exhausted Cole lying on the tables, before he addressed Laura. "There is no law in the area right now, and there are men who would want to insure that Cole doesn't make it. I've sent a telegram to Judge Wilkerson, advising him of the situation." Thornton continued, "I'll stay on to help however I can."

Laura acknowledged his offer, adding, "We must move Cole to the ranch as soon as he is able to travel. Someone put Hawk up to killing Cole, and we need to find out who that person or persons are. Chances are, they didn't trust this job to only one man. Cole is too good." Laura pondered a moment longer and then made a decision. "I must send a telegram myself. There is someone I know who will want to be here as quickly as he is able."

Chapter Fourteen

Converging Trails

Two days later, at the Colorado Territorial Courthouse, Judge Joshua Wilkerson read aloud the telegram from Taylor Thornton. Upon conclusion, he looked across his desk to the tall, dark-haired young man sitting in front of him, "The situation is this: Deputy Marshal Stockton has been seriously wounded in a shootout with a hired murderer known as The Hawk. There is at present, no law to speak of in that part of the territory."

Wilkerson cleared his throat before continuing, "I want you to ride down to Miller's Station to learn the situation firsthand. You'll go incognito, not identifying yourself to anyone. Moreover, I want you to work your way onto Laura Sumner's LS Ranch. Find a way to stay close to Stockton, watch out for him and Miss Sumner. U.S. Marshal Clay Stockton will be on his way there post haste—you can bet your bottom dollar on it."

The judge rolled his eyes upward and pursed his lips as he articulated his thoughts, "I think that Clay will wear out some horseflesh getting to the railroad at Cheyenne. From Cheyenne, he'll come to Denver, grab up a fresh mount and be on his way to the LS Ranch. That should take him about ten to twelve days. I intend that you should be there sizing up the situation before he arrives. Go now with haste."

"Yes, sir," came the man's reply, "I'll change into trail clothes and leave immediately." He rose to leave chambers, quietly closing the door behind himself.

Joshua Wilkerson leaned back in his chair, lit a cigar, and re-read the second telegram from the Colorado Territorial Governor announcing that he had appointed a Territorial Marshal to take over administering the law until Deputy U.S. Marshal Stockton returned to duty. Wilkerson frowned at the particulars contained in the

Governor's message, "I wonder what corrupt lobby faction fabricated this appointment. A territorial marshal, indeed," thought the elder judge. His thoughts leaped through years on the bench, "Isaac Townsend, a known thug and killer—the man is nothing more than a range war specialist. That man, Townsend, has been itching to get into that part of the territory legally, and now he's on his way. Well, two can play at that game, and now I've just sent the *equalizer* into this game of fate. He'll see that justice is done."

* * *

Clay Stockton read the telegram from Laura Sumner and immediately sought out his chief deputy. He found Deputy U.S. Marshal Sandy Merrick at the nearest café and joined him for coffee. "Sandy, I've got to make a trip to Colorado and will probably be gone at least a month."

Merrick studied Clay's worried face a moment, "It sounds serious, Clay. What is it? Is there anything that I can do?"

Clay shook his head, "This is personal. My brother Cole has been seriously wounded in a gunfight. I need to be with him."

Sandy nodded, "I'll take care of things until you get back. You get on the trail."

Clay Stockton considered the information from Miss Sumner as he packed for the trip. His brother Cole was wounded in a shootout. There was no telling what situations would develop without law in the Southern Colorado wilds. Of one thing, he was certain—if someone hired Hawk to gun down his brother, there was sure to be another, or others, out there on the move as well. Cole was too damn good a gun hand to trust their money to just one man to gun Cole down. Someone wanted him out of the way, and they were willing to pay a high price to do it. Two questions remained—who and why? Clay Stockton pondered these questions as he rode hell-bent-for-leather from Bismarck, Dakota Territory toward the railhead at Cheyenne.

* * *

A week after the telegrams were sent to Judge Wilkerson and Clay Stockton, Cole remained an impatient patient of Laura, Taylor and the LS ranch hands. Exhaustion and pain filled his days, causing him to sleep fitfully. Frequently he rambled unintelligible nonsense.

Laura kept a cast iron pot of vegetable stew in beef broth on the stove. Periodically she took a bowl full to his bedside. "You need this stew to build your strength," she scolded, when he balked at eating.

At the end of two weeks, a rider entered the gate of the LS Ranch and rode up to the stables. Judd Ellison stopped his work to warily size up the dark-haired stranger. He was unshaven, his clothes were disheveled and he appeared down on his luck. His horse, however, was obviously well cared for, as was the Colt revolver strapped to his right side.

Judd approached the newcomer, "Who are you and what is your business here?" The man eased the brim of his hat up and smiled a bit, "Name's Bodine, Toby Bodine. I hail from New Mexico, in the Canadian River country, and am in sore need of a job. When I passed through Miller's Station I heard that Miss Sumner might be hiring. I'm into taming wild horses and I'm damn good at it."

The foreman related to Bodine's story. He had been there himself. He nodded, "Step down and tie up your horse. We'll walk over to the main house and speak to Miss Laura. She's the boss and approves all hiring."

Bodine dismounted, and joined Judd Ellison to walk across the ranch yard. They spoke further of Toby's experience while walking. Bodine took in the layout of the ranch yard. Judd paused at the steps of the ranch house. "Sit yourself down on the porch. I'll be right back." Bodine did as bid. Judd knocked on the door, then let himself in.

A few minutes later the foreman returned with Laura Sumner at his side. She sized up Toby then smiled, "Judd tells me that you're looking for a job. He described your experience and that he thinks you would work out. You're hired for now. Stable your mount and find a place in the bunkhouse. Please join us here on the porch for coffee at sunset."

Toby Bodine grinned pleasantly, "Thank you, Miss Sumner. I'm sure you'll be pleased with my work."

The following day, yet another man arrived at the LS Ranch. By contrast, he was a rather handsome Mexican man in his early twenties. Although clean shaven, by the look of his clothes he had traveled a good distance. His mount was spirited and appeared well cared for. He addressed the first man that he encountered. "Buenos tardes, Senor. I am Juan Socorro. I come from below Rio Grande. I look for work with horses. I was just in the ciudad—excuse me, I was just in the town of Miller's Station and they told me at the cantina that I find work here. Who is the boss?"

Eli Johnson spent time as a young ranch hand along the border in Texas. He looked cautiously at this newcomer before responding, "Buenos tardes to you, amigo. You got to habla with the Jefe, the boss. You see that tall man at the corral? That's the foreman, the boss man of this outfit. You ride over there and tell him what you told me. He will habla with you."

Juan Socorro trotted his sorrel gelding to the corrals and greeted the foreman. Judd listened intently while Juan quickly outlined his experience working with horses, and why he was in the Colorado Territory. Juan related, "I know horses. I work for the finest breeders in all of Mexico. I come north, to make a better life. When I go to Miller's Station, I learn that Senorita Sumner has the finest horses in all of the territory. I said, Juan, you need to be here. I want to work for such a rancho."

Judd asked the man to dismount and secure his horse, then invited him to walk with him to the main house. He was impressed when Juan dismounted and only dropped the reins to trail hitch his animal, saying nothing more than, "Wait here, Chico." The sorrel stayed where Juan left him. "I am ready, Senor Judd."

They sauntered across the ranch yard as Juan continued offering information about his home town about one hundred miles south of the border from El Paso. Laura stepped out the porch for fresh air just as the two men approached. Both men removed their hats. Judd introduced Juan and spoke of why the man had traveled far from his home.

Laura gave the latest newcomer a quick once over before she spoke, "Alright, Juan, I'll give you a chance. I need to expand my herd. Your experience is just what we need. You are hired." Laura turned to Judd, "Please introduce Juan to our wranglers and see that he has a place in the bunkhouse."

As Juan and Judd turned to go, Laura added, "Juan, we like to gather here on my porch in the evening for coffee to talk over the day. Please join us."

Juan responded with, "Si Senorita. I do like coffee. I will be here."

* * *

Early that evening, the men gathered on Laura's porch for a cup of strong coffee, cinnamon rolls, and encouraging words. Just as the sun slipped beneath the landscape, a lone rider rode through the ranch gates. The LS Ranch hands grew wary of the new arrival, shifting their holsters nervously and touching revolver butts for reassurance.

When the rider was close enough, Laura beamed because she recognized the lanky form atop the steel gray horse. Laura put her cup down, and moved quickly to the steps of her home to greet an anxious Clay Stockton.

Clay instinctively looked directly at each of the men on the porch as Laura introduced her wranglers. Stockton's eyes stopped for only an instant on one man, with an ever so slight nod, and then Clay asked Laura, "How about some of that coffee, and maybe a plate of your home cooking? I've ridden hard and fast. I'm starved. Can I see Cole?"

Laura replied, "First things first, Cole is sleeping right now, Clay. I'll get a plate of food for you." Jeff Sutton offered to care for Clay's horse, leading it off to the stables. United States Marshal Clay Stockton's arrival insured that a representative of federal law now was present in the area. Laura, Taylor Thornton, and all of her men smiled and breathed a sigh of relief.

* * *

Isaac Townsend had a wry grin on his face as he sat his dapple gray near the edge of Miller's Station. The *Association*, a secretive organization dedicated to open range and unlawful methods, had taken meticulous steps to insure that Townsend be appointed Territorial Marshal by the unwitting governor. They bribed several advisors and lobbyists to support his appointment, insuring the governor that Townsend was the best man to take control of the Miller's Station region.

Issac Townsend carried with him the large sum of money paid him by the Association as payment for services to protect them in their illegal activities.

Yes, Isaac Townsend was the law now, and he could lead a posse in the wrong direction, mislead honest citizens, and sway folks in their decisions to sell their land to the Association as they built their vast cattle empires. Accessing the passes into the New Mexico Territory would be further advantage to their rustling empire. The Association's rustling faction sought to sell stolen stock to the Comanchero who further sold worthy animals to the warring Comanche.

A few trusted deputies, handpicked ruffians by Townsend, would be arriving within the next few hours, and then, Townsend would begin his persuasive methods. He was the law now, and he had taken steps to insure that he would remain the law. He had also arranged to complete the task of ridding the territory of Cole Stockton.

Townsend contemplated the past weeks, "Too bad about Hawk. Hawk was good, but he underestimated Stockton, and he paid for it with his life." Townsend had no such intention of underestimating Stockton. "Stockton will be killed this time, no matter what," Townsend thought with a cynical grin. The executioner was already on Laura Sumner's land. The man was expensive, but would not fail as Hawk had. The next morning would bring the long awaited news of Stockton's demise, and Townsend would prevail as the steadfast law of all the area around Miller's Station.

* * *

All was quiet at the LS Ranch. The midnight hour well past, everyone was sound asleep, except for the lone sentinel stationed with rifle in front of the bunkhouse. The sentry had a clear view of the ranch gate as well as the ranch house.

Unknown to everyone, dark eyes had watched every movement from various positions on the Sumner Ranch throughout the previous week. This technique was the usual manner of the ghost-like figure as he pieced together daily routines. He must strike this very night because too many extra wranglers kept showing up.

From the hill to the side of Laura's house, the lone figure wearing moccasins, crept silently toward the darkened frame of the main ranch building.

Slowly, the shadow worked his way along the ranch house to the front door. Moonlight glinted for a second on the blade of a long knife. A deft movement with the lock, only a slight creak, and the door opened to admit the messenger of death.

The sinister figure moved stealthily across the front room. The reflection of the smoldering coals in the large stone fireplace caste an eerie shadow on the walls as the assailant made his way through the house.

The footsteps stopped at Laura's doorway. The intruder observed her slumber for a few moments. Then, he proceeded further down the hallway to the next room where the recuperating Cole Stockton lay. Both doors stood open so that Laura could hear Cole, should he need her.

The grim figure crept, assured of his direction and, moving swiftly but soundlessly near the bed. His right hand held his weapon of choice, a large Bowie knife. Slowly and silently, he approached the sleeping Cole Stockton. Without remorse he drew the steel blade high above the injured man.

The quiet metallic click of a hammer cocking back broke the silence of the night. Then, the house reverberated with the resultant thunder of a Colt revolver that spit flame and destruction not once, but twice, within the darkness of the house.

Laura flew out of her bed. Groggy, she shook her head to reality, grabbed up her Colt Lightning revolver, and stumbled to the doorway all in one motion. Pausing for a second, she listened intently, before easing to the next doorway where Cole Stockton lay.

The stench of gunpowder stung her nostrils. Her heart pounded in her chest as she took a deep breath before entering the dark room, revolver at the ready. Voices shouted outside the house and suddenly, the front door crashed open to admit Clay Stockton—revolver in hand; an armed Taylor Thornton followed.

Three more men rushed into the house as well. One stopped for moment to strike a match and light the oil lamp in the front room. He carried the lamp cautiously down the hallway and into the room where the injured man lay.

Cole pulled himself up in the bed, a smoking revolver in hand. Laura Sumner stood beside him. A mortally wounded half-breed lay in a heap on the floor near the bed.

Taylor Thornton looked down at the dying Apache's form and swallowed hard. He remembered this man from long ago. The intruder was once an Army scout in his younger years. The man breathed hoarsely, attempting a chant. Thornton leaned down to the man, listening intently. He spoke, "I know this man. This is his death song. He knows that he will die soon."

The eerie chant cut short as the Apache warrior passed into the hands of the Great Spirit. Thornton rummaged the man's pockets. He found money, along with a telegram. Thornton held the crumpled paper to the oil lamp and read it to all in the room. The wire, addressed to John Winslow, provided one name: Cole Stockton. The message was signed: Townsend.

Taylor Thornton sighed before calling out, "May God have mercy on your poor soul." Thornton turned to Cole and the others, "I knew this man, he was known as John Three Horses to all he served. He was once a good tracker and an honest man. I trusted him with my life, back then. I'll bury him myself."

Cole turned to his brother, "Thanks, Clay. Your spare Colt came in handy." He then addressed his friends, "Clay left me his spare while we visited last evening. He knew that I felt naked without one close to hand."

Clay cleared his throat before he spoke, "Cole, we got us a little problem. Isaac Townsend evidently hired this man to murder you. He is now the Territorial Marshal. He's got some pretty rough fellers he calls *deputies* who are going to back him up."

Momentary, Clay looked around the room and grinned, "Toby! Come here. Cole, this is Toby Bodine. Judge Wilkerson sent Toby to help. He's been after Townsend for a long time. It seems that Townsend killed his father much like he arranged for you. Put your badge on now, Toby."

Bodine reached into the pocket of his Levi's and pinned on the silver star of Deputy United States Marshal. He reflected, "Judge Wilkerson sent me to Miller's Station weeks ago to watch the situation. Clay's evaluation is on target. What do you want to do about it?"

"Are you up to it, Cole?" Clay asked of his brother.

"There's no way you can keep me out of it," retorted Cole. "I've grown just a little tired of broth and stews. My stomach says a large beef steak would be mighty tasty come suppertime. All this excitement has made me hungry. Help me up on my horse tomorrow and we'll pay these fellers a visit that they won't long forget. I'm tired of being a target for every hard case with a gun."

Clay looked around the room. "Well, then," he announced, "that makes four of us to meet with Townsend and his henchmen."

"Cinco! Make that five!" came a voice from the doorway. Juan Socorro stepped into the room. He had responded to the sound of gunfire in the house. "I am not a lawman, but I ride for the Senorita. Her home has been violated by theese bad man, and I will protect all for her."

"Swear him in, Clay," directed Cole with his first silly grin since he'd been shot.

"I'm coming too—just try to keep me out of it," added Laura, a determined look on her face.

The five men turned as one to stare at the lady. "You know, you are really beautiful when you are angry," remarked Cole as he gazed directly into her crystal blue eyes. Laura flushed, but held that determined look on her face.

Clay surmised the situation, "Well, it looks a lot like six against six, and that's pretty fair odds."

Sunrise found the group of six saddling up to ride to Miller's Station.

Isaac Townsend and his five deputies had gathered at the jail to discuss their plan to take over the territory, and rake in the spoils of a meticulously planned range war. Their deliberation complete, Townsend suggested that they partake of some liquid refreshment.

They left as a group and walked toward the Star Light Saloon. Mid-way to the saloon, each man stopped in his tracks. Four riders rode into town. Townsend stared in disbelief. He uttered the words, in spite of himself, that sent chills running down his spine, "Stockton—he's alive."

He and his men watched as the four men reined in, dismounted, and tied up at hitching posts on either side of the street. The newcomers spread out across the wide dusty street, as they walked toward Townsend and his men.

Clay Stockton issued the challenge, "Townsend! You and all of your friends are under arrest for conspiracy to commit murder."

Townsend and his men searched the faces of the four spread out in front of them, and weighed their chances. Likely, someone was going to die. The two factions now faced each other across an area of twenty yards. Townsend took special note that three of the four adversaries wore silver stars of authority.

The youngest one, dark-haired and about twenty-two years old, glared at Townsend. A memory slipped into the forefront of his mind. Yes, he had known those eyes. He knew that face, long ago. That would be Jack Bodine, Sheriff of the Canadian River country in New Mexico. This youngster would be his son bent on revenge.

Townsend was not sure whether he could take Cole Stockton, even though he seemed to favor his left shoulder, but he was sure as the Devil that he could take the kid. He mouthed the words that sealed his fate, "Bodine, I'm going to shoot you down like I killed your old man."

Suddenly, Townsend opened the ball, as his hand swept down for the pistol at his belt. At that moment, everyone reached for weapons. Revolvers flashed in the sunlight. Flame and hot death spit from blackened muzzles. Gunsmoke filled the air amid sharp cracks.

Larry Mohra never knew what hit him. Clay Stockton's hand flashed, and the muzzle of his Colt exploded, sending burning lead straight into Mohra's heart. He was dead before he hit the ground.

Zeb Colter exchanged shots with Taylor Thornton and Clay Stockton. He lost. Thornton was hit in the side, but managed to put two rounds into Colter who staggered backward with each bullet. Then Clay Stockton's second bullet slammed into him and he fell to the ground.

Hurley James and Kid Langley both aimed for Cole Stockton. Cole's Peacemaker seemed to leap into his hand. The pistols of both men had just cleared leather when Cole's first bullet split the air taking James in the center of his body. Langley's revolver spit flame and he stared wide-eyed when his first round tore through Stockton's left shirtsleeve, then smacked into a building behind Stockton.

Stockton's Colt cracked again. A searing fire burned into Langley's body. He looked down in fear at his groin to find the spreading red stain. It hurt like fire, yet he leveled his revolver for a second shot at Cole Stockton.

Cole watched him only a split second, and then shot Langley again—straight in the chest. Langley slammed to the ground, eyes staring at the blue sky.

Luke Wimberly turned and ran down the street. He wanted no part of these federal marshals. He was near the livery stable when two armed figures appeared before him. One was a woman, her face set with determination. The other was a young Mexican. Both held rifles at the ready.

Wimberly grinned wickedly. He could take any woman and a Mexican. He reached for his holstered gun and instantly two Winchester bullets cut him down. The last thing he saw was the puff of smoke from each of the two rifle muzzles.

Toby Bodine and Issac Townsend faced each other with death in their eyes. Townsend lined his revolver on Bodine. At the same moment, Bodine's weapon spit flame. The spinning hot lead hit Townsend with an ugly thud, jerking him backward on impact. He instantly thumbed a round at Bodine, snarling, "I'm too mean to die!" His bullet struck Bodine in the waist.

The young Deputy Marshal faltered as he fired again, and again, and again just as fast as he could. Townsend's body jerked with each hit, crumbling grotesquely to the ground. Even in death, the look of hatred etched on Townsend's face.

Bodine slipped to the ground holding his waist, a dark patch of red spreading along his shirt. Clay Stockton was immediately beside the young man, leaning over to tear open Toby's shirt. Clay yanked his own bandana off and pressed it against the wound. A grin spread across Clay's face, "First time shot, huh? W-e-l-l, ya got him badder than he got you—and he ain't complaining none."

Toby looked straight at Clay, and he laughed against the pain in his side. "I sort of over did it—didn't I?" Clay chuckled, "Well, kid, I'd say you kilt him about twice over."

Laura Sumner and Juan Socorro joined Cole to help Taylor Thornton up from the ground. Thornton leaned against Juan for balance. Cole reached out to place his arm around Laura's waist. He gazed into her eyes, announcing "I'm proud of you, Laura, and always will be."

Their arms were around one other as they kissed. Taylor Thornton grinned widely as he remarked, "Yessir! just like I said before—hot as a raging prairie fire." Cole and Laura turned as one to face Thornton. A knowing smile spread across both their faces.

Silence hovered over Main Street in Miller's Station while gun smoke aimlessly dispersed into the morning air. Townspeople emerged from hiding places to view the deadly scene. The notorious Territorial Marshal and his deputies lay dead, a grim reminder that justice eventually comes to those who wield guns with evil in their hearts.

Chapter Fifteen

Prelude to a Dangerous Trail

A year had passed since the shootout at Miller's Station. Except for periodic aches in my left shoulder, especially when ole man winter raised his icy breath across the Colorado, I felt fit as a fiddle.

The citizens of Miller's Station elected themselves an honest sheriff by the name of J.C. Kincaid. J.C. and I formed a good relationship. We respected each other, working jointly on numerous cases. I grew to like and trust this man, Kincaid.

Spring came once again to the southern Colorado. The air filled with fresh scents of wild flowers and pine. As snow in the high country melted, the rivers, creeks, and lakes teemed with clear, cold running water, and fresh trout. Livestock shed their winter coats.

Local ranchers formed roundups to gather their herds where they would count new additions. The Sumner Horse Ranch was no exception. Laura waited anxiously to see the results of breeding her black stallion, Sultan, to select mares. She moved everywhere at once, giving direction to her wranglers, seeing to repairs on stables, corrals, and holding pens. Her tasks to complete included: new ropes to make, stalls to clean, leather to mend, and saddles to soap down. Laura presided in the thick of it all from sun up to sun down.

I, on the other hand, was primarily left to my own devices, thoughts, and meandering. Now was no time cuddle with Laura; she stayed too busy running her ranch. I admired the way that she took charge and it goes without saying that her hired hands admired her also. She was an expert horsewoman, she could shoot with more accuracy than most men, and she held no qualms about rolling up her sleeves to dig into the work at hand.

Spring also brought challenges to the wilds of the Lower Colorado. Farmers would begin preparing their ground for spring planting. Young men would be eyeing the girls. Things picked up as well in my line of business. Indian factions would be on the move; however, foremost on my mind, remained the fact that hard elements would once again crawl out of their winter hideouts to prey on those who did not live by the gun.

Preventing such behavior was my calling. The name Cole Stockton seemed to strike a note of caution with those that rode the lonely, wild trails between the Mexican and the Canadian borders. It had been said, that I am respected by some, feared by others, and despised by many, because of the star that I wear—Deputy United States Marshal.

* * *

Much farther south, it looked to be another typical hot, dry and dusty day in the little Mexican town one hundred miles south of El Paso, Texas. Manuel Vargas sat smoking a cigarillo on a bench in front of his small adobe, as he watched his young daughter Emilita run excitedly up the path toward their home.

"Papa! A letter came from Juan. He is returning to me. Remember, Papa? He promised that he would find a good job in the north and would come back to me. He has a good job on a horse ranch in the Colorado Territory. See, Papa, I told you he would be back for me. Now, I will be free of Raul."

Manuel smiled sadly at his daughter. "How lovely she is," he thought. "She has always loved this man, Juan Socorro, but she must marry Raul, the son of the ranchero." Manuel had promised his daughter, this lovely young girl, to Raul in order to allow his family to live in peace on the ranchero's land. Emilita was their only ticket to survival, such as it was.

The ranchero, Enrique Delgado Garcia de Marza, owned the land for one hundred miles in each direction, by a centuries old grant of the King of Spain. The faded parchment document hung framed on the wall of the great room in de Marza's hacienda. It identified the de Marza family lineage and their claim to the land.

"Juan Socorro may come back to Mexico, but he will never marry my Emilita," thought Manuel. He knew of the danger. If news spread that Juan was coming for his daughter, there would be danger in every corner of the land. The ranchero would learn his every movement and have Juan hunted down and killed. The ranchero was an evil man. Perhaps he would imprison Juan in his silver mine, never to be seen or heard of again.

Manuel knew about the silver mines. He had witnessed strangers come into his village, enjoy a few drinks of tequila at the cantina, and then disappear. The ranchero reined as a most powerful man.

Manuel pondered the situation as he watched smoke waft lazily from his cigarillo, then encircle his head. He wished that there was some other way. He wished the best for his daughter, yet she was eighteen now and promised to the ranchero's eldest son. Their union would bring security for all his family as well as a life of ease for Emilita.

Emilita had rebuffed Raul's attentions in the past, yet Raul was as aggressive as he was flamboyant. This handsome caballero would inherit all his father's holdings one day. He would inherit, however, only if he abided by the wishes of his elder. The elder wished Raul to marry Emilita. The elder de Marza had watched Emilita over the years as she matured into a desirable senorita. She was young and beautiful and surely she would produce many grandchildren for the patriarch.

* * *

Juan Socorro sat across the kitchen table drinking coffee as he explained to Laura Sumner his plans of marriage. He spoke of his sweetheart Emilita and of his promise to return to Mexico to marry her. The young wrangler had saved most everything that Laura paid him during the past year. At last, he had enough to marry his beloved and return with her to the Lower Colorado.

Laura listened with her heart and a twinkle in her eyes. She liked this handsome young horseman. Juan had performed well as her wrangler and he certainly knew horses. She pondered his plans as a vision of horse breeding swept through her mind. "What if," Laura thought, "what if, Juan might purchase a fine stallion from a ranchero in Mexico? Would it further refine her breed of horses?"

Laura knew that some of the finest horses in the west came from Mexican stock. The journey Juan planned for marriage presented the opportunity for Laura to expand her horse ranch.

Laura began, "Juan, I'm eager to meet Emilita. I know that you will be happy together here on the ranch. We all look forward to your return. I do have a favor to ask of you."

Juan looked questioningly at Laura. "What is it that you wish, Senorita Laura?"

Laura continued, "Would you look into a purchase for me? I would like to buy a Mexican stallion for our herds. I want you to be my representative and purchase this stallion. I will give you a one thousand dollar bank draft. I trust your judgment. We will anxiously await your return."

Juan's face lit up with the task Laura offered, "Senorita Laura, you have made me so very happy. My Emilita will love living here on this ranch. I am more than happy to serve you in this way. Yes, I know of a Ranchero who has many fine horses. His stock is some of the finest in all of Mexico. You will do well to buy one of his stallions. I will do this for you."

Socorro pondered for a moment, "I should be back within two months. I will bring my Emilita, and a fine stallion for you."

The next morning, Juan Socorro mounted up and with a gallant wave, turned his horse toward the south and Mexico.

I stood on the porch with Laura and waved farewell along with her. I thought that Laura's latest venture represented a good business move. I had spent time along the border and had seen, first hand, some of the finest horseflesh around. It was little wonder that the Comanche routinely raided into Mexico in search of those horses.

As I watched Juan ride into the horizon, call it a premonition, a shiver rippled through my body as he disappeared from sight. I didn't know it then, but I would make a trip into the desert of Mexico. The lives of several people would hinge on my journey.

* * *

Two days later, with nothing much to do, I rode along with Laura's roundup crew. I stayed close to the main camp and that coffee pot. There is nothing like the taste of fresh coffee over a campfire to set a man thinking. Laura was a good woman, and I surely felt thankful for that. We had been together now, going on three years and had been through the mill together for sure.

At times, I wished we had tied the knot, yet there were times I felt glad that we had not married. All in all, it seemed to work out. Laura had her ranch to care for; I had my marshaling to do.

I'd said it many times, that I didn't want a woman to wonder when I rode away each time, whether or not I would be coming back. Laura understood this philosophy, and that is what brought us closer together, I believe. I didn't have to explain anything to her. Each time I returned, we held each other close, gazed into each other's eyes, and let the smoldering fire of our souls take charge.

Many times on lonely trails, I felt the surging warmth of her arms around me. Those visions saw me through some mighty rough scrapes with Old Man Death. Yes, it was the Almighty who looked out for me as well.

As I sat close to the campfire sipping coffee with Warrior nearby, Laura came a-whooping into camp. She slid off Mickey in the midst of a dust swirling halt, then began to dance like a darn fool kid. That woman had the biggest smile on her face I ever saw. Her crystal blue eyes sparkled.

I took in her excitement, then blurted out, "Laura, just what the devil has gotten into you? Have you been chewing loco weed or what?"

She looked down at me with a big grin. Then, she exclaimed, "Oh, Cole! I have just come from the far end of the range. We found Sultan and his herd, and there are ten beautiful foals. They are s-o-o-o-o beautiful, lively, and strong. W-e-l-l, you have just got to see them. I am so happy I could kiss the roundup cook. My dream of having an extraordinary horse ranch is taking shape."

Smiling, I responded to her, "I'm truly happy for you, Laura. I hope that there are many more horses to come."

The next thing I knew she sat on my lap, then threw her arms around my neck and whispered in my ear. "Cole Stockton, I love you, and you are about to get the biggest kiss you've ever had."

Her arms went around my waist tightly. Suddenly, we tumbled into the grass. Warrior stepped sideways and back, looking at us as if we were senseless. Our arms entwined, we embraced as she planted kisses on me like no time before. I enjoyed it. Like I said, she was *excited* about those foals.

Chapter Sixteen

Juan's Dilemma

After twelve days on the trail from the Lower Colorado, through the New Mexico Territory, and into Texas, Juan Socorro arrived in El Paso. It was early evening, the time that this wild border town came alive.

Pianos clanked rowdy tunes in the many saloons and gambling halls. Late night shoot-outs happened frequently here. On the Rio Grande side of town, the music was different in the Mexican cantinas. Mariachi music dominated.

Amongst his countrymen, Juan Socorro found a quiet cantina near the place where he would cross the Rio Grande. Weary, he turned his bay horse into the hitching rack. He dismounted stiffly, stomping his feet a few times to get circulation moving. The vaquero allowed his mount to drink of the tepid trough water before securing the reins to the post.

Juan entered the cantina and then stepped a bit to the right, letting his eyes become accustomed to the dimness of the bar area. A guitar duo played softly in one corner. He glanced around the room to see men seated around roughly hewn tables drinking tequila and playing Cooncan, otherwise known as Mexican Rummy. Another table hosted a poker game. Still, others sat around the cantina talking quietly while sipping glasses of beer and tequila.

A couple of rough-looking men leaned against the bar. A bottle of tequila stood between them. They pondered in silence this new arrival who appeared to be Mexican but dressed as an Americano, except for his sombrero.

Juan walked casually up to the bar. A mustachioed bartender looked him over for a few seconds before questioning, "Qué quiere?"

"Un cerveza, por favor," responded Juan. Within moments, the man set a mug of cool beer in front of the young caballero. Juan placed a silver dollar on the bar in payment.

The bartender pondered the coin, before asking, "You have worked in the north for a while?" Juan nodded as he slowly sipped on his beer. Then Juan inquired of a quiet place for the night. The bartender suggested a small two-story adobe guesthouse down the street. He mentioned that a widow ran the place and could use the business.

Juan thanked the man, "Gracias, amigo." He finished his beer, stepped outside the cantina, and walked his horse down the street to the guesthouse.

The building was shabby to say the least, but honest in its accommodations. Juan got a room for the night, stabling his bay in a lean-to stall behind the building. Once situated, Juan lay back on the single bunk, closed his eyes, and dreamed about the next day when he would ride once more into his homeland—Mexico. A smile spread across his face as he dreamed of Emilita. She ran toward him, her arms outstretched to him. He dreamed of her smile and her warmth enveloped him.

The next morning, the young caballero rose at first light. He washed up, changed his clothes and walked down the stairs to a breakfast of huevoes rancheros and flour tortillas with a spicy sauce. To Juan, it felt good to be back where they made such meals as this. When he was ready, he saddled up the bay. He spoke gently to the horse, relating all about the country that they would pass through on their way to Emilita. Finally, he swung easily into the saddle and made his way toward the Rio Grande.

The river was narrow and quite shallow on this day. Juan rode into the slow moving water, stopping at about mid-point. Looking over his shoulder to the United States, he thought of the new life he had made for himself and soon for Emilita in the Lower Colorado. A shudder of doubt surged through him, yet he didn't know why. In a moment he shrugged it off and heeled his mount toward the opposite shore.

Climbing out of the water and onto the bank on the other side, Juan was in Mexico. He smiled, thinking, "Only one hundred miles further to Emilita. I will be there within the week." He touched spur to his mount, moving into an easy trot. Engrossed in thoughts of his love, he failed to sense the watchful eyes from a nearby arroyo that followed his every move.

* * *

Ricardo Alvarez drew deep on the cigarillo. He held the hot smoke that filled his lungs for a moment before exhaling. The man watched the smoke drift on the warm current of air and smiled with a crooked grin. Raul paid him handsomely to watch for this man, Juan, and now he had returned to Mexico.

Ricardo knew Juan. They had grown up in the same village and had been classmates at the mission school. Ricardo was always jealous of Juan. Juan had the knack of working with horses, a trade well respected in the states of Mexico. Juan was respected, even by adults, for his skills.

Ricardo, on the other hand, had bullied his way through life, taking up with men of dubious repute. He lived with the gun, selling his services to anyone who would pay him to use it. Ricardo wanted to kill Juan, but orders from Raul were explicit. He would sight Socorro, then follow him for a while. He would let Raul know of Juan's movements once in Mexico.

Raul would deal with Juan in his own manner. Ricardo grinned with an evil thought. He knew Raul's manner, and it was a fate worse than death. Raul would send Juan to the silver mines where he would be beaten and broken into a mere shell of a man. There, he would be kept alive only to work, then subsequently die in the darkness of the mine. His burial would be a lonely unmarked grave.

Ricardo watched Juan ride south until he became a speck on the horizon. Ricardo then mounted his dun horse and followed Juan's tracks into the sandy, cactus-dotted Mexican desert. He would follow for one day before racing ahead to inform Raul that Juan Socorro would arrive soon.

* * *

At mid-afternoon of the third day in Mexico, Juan Socorro rode through his home village. He had been away for little over a year yet the village had not changed. He thought, "This village has been here many years and will be the same for many more. I will take Emilita away from here. She will have a new life in the Colorado." He headed toward the adobe house of his sweetheart Emilita.

Juan grew concerned when he arrived at the adobe. Several saddle horses and a wagon stood at the hitching rack in front of the gate. Nonetheless, he was there to see his love. He dismounted, stepped through the gate and into the yard. At the door of the adobe, Juan removed his sombrero. He reached out to knock.

The wooden door opened suddenly, and five rough men pushed Juan back out into the yard, surrounding him. This *welcome* took Juan by surprise. Crowding him, the men seized his revolver and belt knife. Then, they held him fast by both arms. The men said nothing, but grinned at him with knowing sneers upon their faces.

"Who are you? What do you want of me?" Juan questioned.

Just then, another man dressed in the fine clothes of a gentleman stepped out into the yard. He grinned wickedly at Juan Socorro as he nodded his head affirmatively. "So! Juan Socorro. You think that you can ride back into Mexico, into my territory, and take my woman, take my wife-to-be? I think not, Juan Socorro. I think that you have come back to this village to die."

Raul moved close to Juan and stared directly into his puzzled eyes. Juan did not understand what the ranchero's son meant. He started to speak. Raul moved quickly and silenced him with a vicious blow to Juan's right temple using the handle of his quirt. Juan Socorro slumped to the ground, unconscious.

Emilita burst through the door of the adobe. Her eyes were red and swollen, tears streaked her cheeks. She attempted to run to Juan, but her father held her back, pulling her toward the adobe.

The young senorita turned against her father, screaming, "Father, how could you? You told Raul of Juan's coming. How could you? They have hurt him. Help him, Father. Help Juan or I will never speak to you again!"

Emilita twisted suddenly and broke free of her father. She dashed to Juan, leaning down to touch his face. Raul grabbed her and flung her backward. She fell to the ground, the breath knocked out of her.

Manuel Vargas realized what he had been party to. He felt shamed in the face of his daughter. Raul truly was a monster and he had hurt his beloved daughter. Anger flushed Manuel's cheeks as he rushed forward to grab Raul from behind.

The younger man turned quickly, knocking the older man to the ground. He turned his quirt on Emilita's father, beating him unmercifully with knotted leather thongs. Blood seeped through the old man's shirt where the thongs sliced the fabric.

"Take this old fool to the silver mines also," growled Raul. "Both will suffer the wrath of Raul. Take the girl to the hacienda. She will remain there until the wedding date is set and the ceremony performed."

Raul's men complied. They tied Juan Socorro and the old man across their saddles and rode toward the *pit of no return*. Two others forced a tearful Emilita into the wagon and drove off toward Rancho de Marza.

* * *

Hours later, Juan Socorro opened his eyes. His head ached like no time before. Raising both hands to his head, he felt the dried blood at this temple. He leaned back against a cold wall in an effort to steady himself. Juan struggled to focus in the dim light of a damp dungeon cell. After a few minutes, Juan moved his body to hear the rattle of chains. He shook his head to clear it, only then looking at his feet. His ankles were shackled together with chains.

Juan heard another outcry of pain. His eyes searched the opposite dark corner. A figure lay crumpled in the corner on the stone floor. Minutes passed before Juan recognized Manuel Vargas, Emilita's father. He had been severely beaten, shackled, and dumped into the cell along with Juan.

Juan cautiously moved to the old man's side. He gently turned him over, brushing dirt from Manuel's face. "I brought this evil upon us," whispered the old man hoarsely. "May God have mercy on me. We will both die here in this mine."

"No! We won't." said Juan with a fiery, determined voice. "These people don't know what they have done. I have friends in the Colorado Territory. They will come for me. They will come for me and it will be like the Angel of Death descending upon these wicked ones. Mark my words."

* * *

A week passed without Emilita knowing the fate of her father or Juan Socorro. The young woman was despondent, often fearing for her life at the wrath of Raul de Marza. She lived continually under the scrutiny of his trusted servants except at night in the room where she dressed and slept. Even then, a guard stood outside her door. Tears flooded her face as she prayed for the safety of her father and Juan.

On this night before retiring, Emilita stood in front of the immense wooden wardrobe that held her clothes. Raul had sent servants to the adobe to bring all of her clothes to the hacienda. Suddenly, she remembered the letter. Recalling the day she wept with joy when Juan's letter arrived, Emilita frantically searched through the wardrobe and finally found the floral print with pockets that she had worn. The letter remained in the pocket. It bore a return address.

Juan Socorro
C/O Sumner Ranch
Miller's Station, Colorado Territory
United States of America

Surely, she thought, those people in Colorado could help. Juan had written that he had many friends at the ranch and that they helped each other in times of trouble. By candlelight Emilita sat at the small table near her bed to write a simple plea for help. She sealed it in an envelope, addressing it exactly as Juan had handwritten his return,

Sumner Ranch
Miller's Station, Colorado Territory
United States of America

How would she post the plea? As a prisoner within the walls of the rancho, she was watched continuously. Whom could she trust? Who would deliver this envelope to the post office and post it without suspicion? She must carry the envelope with her, hiding it within her clothes, until she found the most trusted person.

A few days later Emilita found that someone. She selected Pedro, a young boy of fourteen. Pedro was the goat herder who brought fresh milk to the hacienda each day. Pedro liked the young senorita and was kind to her. He often made a special stop in the evening to bring her a cup of fresh goat's milk. She and Pedro would stand in the garden and talk while she drank it.

On this particular evening, Emilita drank her goat's milk more slowly than usual. She seemed very nervous as she passed the cup back to Pedro. With the cup, she also slipped the envelope, along with a peso to the young man.

The young goat herder looked directly into her eyes and saw the spark of hope. He nodded ever so slightly, swallowing hard, as he left the rancho. Emilita prayed that no one had seen the exchange and that Pedro would meet no harm as he mailed her letter.

The following evening, Pedro again brought her a cup of fresh milk. They stood in the garden again while she drank. Her eyes were anxious, but Pedro just smiled at her and spoke pleasantries as usual.

When she returned the cup the slight wink from the young man let her know that the letter had been dispatched. She touched Pedro's hand ever so slightly, acknowledging his message. Now, she could only wait. Colorado was a long way from Mexico.

Chapter Seventeen

A Mission Most Urgent

More than a week after Emilita's letter was posted, Laura Sumner opened the unusual envelope postmarked from Mexico. She read the note. Her eyes grew wide as anger spread across her face. The lady rancher turned quickly on her heels and rushed out to the front porch. Her arm curled around a column as she yelled to her foreman, "Judd! Judd! Come here! I need you right away."

Judd Ellison heard Laura's voice from across the ranch yard and trotted quickly to her side. He immediately saw her deep furrowed brow and questioned, "Something wrong, Miss Laura?"

"You bet there is, Judd! I need you to go find Cole Stockton right away. There is trouble—trouble that only he knows how to handle. You find him, Judd, and you tell him that it's urgent that I talk with him."

Judd ran to the stable, saddled his horse and within moments was on the road to Miller's Station and Cole Stockton.

* * *

I sat swapping yarns with newly elected Sheriff J.C. Kincaid over a cup of his sorry coffee when Judd Ellison rode up to the jail like the very Devil himself was on his heels. He slid that sorrel of his to a dust swirling halt, jumped out of the saddle, and was through the jailhouse door before you could say, "Who flung the dung?"

Judd's jaw was set as he related Laura's instructions, "Cole, Laura said to come and get you immediately. There's trouble. In fact, she put it this way—there's trouble that only Cole Stockton knows how to handle."

My first remark was, "I should've known. Things have been just too quiet around here. O.K., Judd, let's get on back to the ranch." I turned to the sheriff, "J.C., That has got to be the worst coffee you ever made. Where in the hell did you get them beans?"

J.C. grinned sheepishly when he replied, "Hell, Cole. It ain't the coffee beans. An old prospector told me the other day that coffee tastes a lot better if you put a little gunpowder in it. Well, I cracked a bullet and poured gunpowder in the grounds. It is a trifle bitter—ain't it?"

"J.C., I think you're loco. You need a rest. Why don't you wire Toby Bodine. Tell him to come on down here. Go fishing up at the lake for a couple of days. As a matter of fact, wire Toby and tell him to come on down here anyway. I'm going to take a trip. I can feel it in my bones."

Ellison and I wasted no time riding back to the Sumner Ranch. Laura showed me the note from Mexico. Lord, was she angry! Not only was Juan Socorro in trouble, but there was the matter of the one thousand dollar bank draft that she gave him to purchase a stud horse.

"And," snapped Laura, "if Juan is imprisoned in a silver mine fortress, then where is his horse? He branded that bay with the LS brand even though I gave it to him as a bonus, and that adds horse stealing to the situation as well."

Laura paced in silence several minutes before she turned to me, "Cole, you know what I want. I want my wrangler back. I want either my money back or a worthy stallion, and—I want justice in this matter."

I could see that Laura had more to say. In the back of my mind the thought came, "Hell hath no fury as a woman scorned."

A moment later, she kicked a chair leg, then stomped her foot. "Dammit! I wish that I could just take all my boys and ride down there. I'd read those people the law of the land." That kind of revenge wasn't possible, and she knew it. Then she fell silent. Minutes ticked by before Laura looked into my eyes. This time she spoke calmly, "Will you go, Cole?"

I nodded affirmatively as I said, "I'll leave first thing in the morning. I like Juan as well. There will be hell to pay for any harm to him."

That evening, Laura and I sat together on the settee in front of the fireplace. She remained quiet, but I knew what was on her mind as she leaned against my shoulder, her way of telling me that she would miss me and to be careful.

With my arm around her, I thought of the trip into Mexico myself. It would most certainly be dangerous. Was I still good enough? A couple of telegrams would go out in the morning. I knew a couple of old codgers who might like some excitement, and I could use a bit of help with this matter.

The next morning my duffle was packed with extra clothes and necessities for the trail. I checked my Winchester rifle, honed my belt knife, and insured the workings of my second Colt revolver. With the cartridge belt filled and extra ammunition in my saddlebags, my gear was placed by the front door for travel.

Laura worked in the kitchen preparing her part of my send off. I caught the aroma of rich, black coffee brewing as well as the aroma of fresh biscuits and sizzling bacon. She would send me off with a breakfast to behold.

I stepped into the kitchen dressed for travel. Laura nodded approval with my attire, recalling me dressed like this too many times before. My mind was already on the wild trails before me.

She motioned to the table. Momentarily, she placed two plates piled with fried eggs, crisp bacon, fried potatoes, and a passel of biscuits between us. She poured us each a cup of coffee before sitting opposite me. When those crystal blue eyes met mine, I knew I would return. "You can bet on it," I mused to myself. "I wouldn't miss a homecoming to this woman if my very life depended on it." Well, it did.

We made small talk as we ate. I gazed into her eyes. I was burning her impression into my soul and she knew it. When I stood, she handed me a sizable parcel of beef jerky and biscuits. She knew me pretty well.

We walked to the porch together to find all of Laura's wranglers gathered there. I could see it on each face. Their friend was in trouble down in Mexico. They all wished that they could go with me.

I turned to Laura and she melted into my arms for a long kiss. The ranch hands respectfully studied their boots and the ground. When we parted, I turned to the wranglers and said, "I know your feelings about Juan, boys. I know each of you want to go, too. This is a job for someone who knows the breed of men that hold him prisoner—someone who can be just as hard as they are. There will be friends riding into Mexico me. Rest assured that I'll return with Juan."

I swung into the saddle, waved farewell, then pointed Warrior toward my first stop. I planned to be at the Rio Grande in about eight to ten days. Once in El Paso, all hell would break loose. I stopped at the telegraph office in Miller's Station, sending two telegrams before heading for the south passes.

* * *

Taylor Thornton sat on the porch of his ranch house near Lincoln, New Mexico Territory watching the lone rider boiling dust toward him. He recognized the young man as the telegraph runner from town by the time the kid skidded his horse to a halt in front of his house. "Charlie," he said, "you seem to be in quite a hurry. What's the problem?"

Charlie answered excitedly. "Mr. Thornton, I got a telegram here for you. It's marked urgent, and by God, Mr. Thornton, you never told us that you knew Cole Stockton personally. Why, he's got to be the fastest man with a gun I ever heard tell of. This wire is from him. He wants you to meet him in El Paso as fast as you can fork a bronc and ride on over there."

Taylor took the wire from Charlie, read it quickly, and jumped up from his chair. He leaped to the bottom step and yelled to his foreman, "Bill! Have a wrangler saddle up my horse, Buck, and bring him to the house."

He turned and dashed into the house. "Cassie!" he shouted to his wife. "Pack me up some traveling grub. I'm going to El Paso." Taylor wasted no time as he hastened into the bedroom to pack his duffle.

A short time later, Cassie watched Taylor open his gun case. He grabbed his gunbelt, filled the loops with cartridges and strapped it around his waist. Gripping his favorite Colt revolver, he slipped it into the holster. Last, he removed the Winchester 73 from the case, checking it carefully.

Cassie Thornton hadn't seen her husband this excited since the time that he took that young horse Warrior up to the Colorado Territory to Cole Stockton. She had a concerned look as he donned his coat and Stetson. He was ready. She had read the telegram also, and knew he had to go.

She walked out to the porch with him just as a wrangler brought his saddled buckskin horse to the porch. His ranch hands were there as well as to see him off when Cassie handed Taylor a travel sack of jerky and biscuits. He gave her a hug and a quick peck of a kiss. "You take care, Taylor. I know you have to go, but, you be careful."

Taylor nodded. He turned to his hands, "You boys watch out for Cassie. I'll be back. You can count on it. And, then he put boot to stirrup, swung into the saddle and pointed Buck southwest. He hesitated at the gate, turning the buckskin to face Cassie one last time. Suddenly, he reared the gelding and waved his Stetson at his wife.

Cassie loved his flamboyant farewell. She had tears in her eyes, but they were tears of gladness. Taylor needed something like this to put the life he once had back. They were fairly well off and the ranch was going well with a young foreman running the show. Taylor sometimes felt he was out to pasture. He had been fidgety the past several months. Now, his spirit responded as that of a young man called to duty. Cassie smiled. This man was her knight in shining armor off on his quest. She felt happy for him.

*   *   *

In the mid-afternoon at Penny Cooper's Boarding House in Fort Stockton, Texas, three former Texas Rangers sat at the kitchen table sipping coffee as they played Gin Rummy.

Penny, the petite auburn haired proprietress, was busy putting together a false apple pie for the evening dessert. Puffs of flour streaked her cheeks and spatters of ground cinnamon formed an uneven pattern across her apron.

The front door of the boarding house opened and heavy footsteps charged into the parlor, through the dining room, and finally into the kitchen. The men looked up from their card game. Donny Watson, the telegraph runner, stood there out of breath.

"Well, what's got you all up in a dither, Donny?" questioned Justin Cooper, Penny's husband.

The teenage telegraph runner stammered, "Coop, I got a telegram here for you and it's marked urgent. I looked at the sender's name and by God, Coop, it's from Cole Stockton, the gunfighter. Do you know him? I mean, Cole Stockton. Gee Coop, I wish that I could meet him."

Hearing the name, Justin Cooper stood, Josh Farley stood, and Jim Slater stood. Penny Ann Miller Cooper turned at the name to look at her husband. Without a word, Coop took the telegram from Donny and read it. A broad grin spread across his face, and his eyes lit up.

Penny moved over to her husband and read the wire herself. It was from Stockton alright and he needed help. He wanted Coop, Josh, and Jim to meet him in El Paso as soon as they could get to the border town.

All three men had left the Texas Rangers within the past year. Without the excitement of tracking down outlaws, the three hung around Penny's kitchen, played cards, and told yarns. The three companions were getting on Penny's nerves more than they knew. She had wished that some circumstance would come about to call them back to active duty with the Rangers. She wished for anything that would lift their spirits and get the brightness back into their eyes. Cole Stockton's request was it!

Coop turned to Penny and said, "Honey. Pack my trail bag. We're headed to El Paso. I don't know much yet, but when Cole needs help, we are the ones to go. Glory be! We are back on the trails, boys!"

The three friends scrambled upstairs to prepare for their journey. Penny Cooper danced around the kitchen as she put on fresh coffee, rolled out biscuits, and packed up a passel of sliced beef, ham, and cheese. The *boys* had become young wild men again. The gleam of adventure shined in their eyes. Their old friend Cole Stockton had need of them and by Jove, they were going to his aid.

Chapter Eighteen

The Gathering

Some ten days later, I rode slowly down Main Street of El Paso, Texas. I turned Warrior into the hitching rack at a hotel whose proprietor was American. The town had grown somewhat since my last visit. What with new store fronts and cantinas along with family adobes, I estimated that the local population numbered about a thousand folks. There was no telling what the transient population added.

I dismounted wearily, allowing Warrior to seek the life-giving water from the trough. After several minutes, I stroked his neck, then looped the reins loosely over the hitching rail.

Stepping up onto the hotel boardwalk, I shuffled into the lobby where four men sat in easy chairs reading various newspapers supplied by the hotel. This coveted reading material arrived weekly on the stagecoach for the hotel guests.

I moved over to the registration desk. The neatly dressed clerk peered from behind his wire-rimmed spectacles to look me over. I saw and sensed his distaste for me. I was sweaty and dusty from head to toe. I empathized with him. I was not a well groomed gentleman myself, but I let him know that I needed a room and could pay for it. He turned the register toward me for me to sign my name.

Like most hotel clerks in the West, he scrutinized the name. I noticed that as he peered at my signature, his eyes widened. When he looked up at me again, a certain respect had overtaken his face.

"Yes, sir, Marshal Stockton. You will be in room 204."

I took the key from the clerk's unsteady hand while I instructed him to have Warrior taken to the livery and to stable him for the night. I turned toward the stairs, then stopped to glance around the lobby.

What a sight for sore eyes! All of my friends had showed up. I nodded towards the cantina entrance and one by one they headed in that direction. Checking out my room on the second floor, I saw that it faced the main street. The accommodations would do for one night's rest. Once I had washed my hands and face in the porcelain basin, I went down to the saloon to join my friends.

Justin Cooper, Josh Slater, and Jim Farley were at a back table. I joined Taylor Thornton at the bar. "Hello, Taylor. Glad you could make it. Let's grab a couple of beers and join some other friends of mine at that back table."

Once seated, I made introductions around the table and we sipped our beers. Having relaxed a few minutes, I leaned forward across the table and filled them in.

"Well, boys, I've got a good one. One of Laura Sumner's best wranglers went down into Mexico about one hundred miles from here, and got himself in a bad situation. I understand he is being held prisoner in a silver mine. As you would expect, he is forced to work or die, and I doubt he will ever see daylight again unless we get him out. I understand that at least forty gunmen—riders to the ranchero, enforce this prison."

My friends leaned closer to me as I continued, "I intend to break him out, mete out some six gun justice, and head back to El Paso with him, his sweetheart, and her father, as well as a couple of horses, and some missing money."

I let my friends ponder that for a moment while I downed my beer. I concluded the conversation with, "I don't particularly care who gets in the way, and I don't care what it takes, or how many I have to shoot to do it. I will get him out. These men are vicious, and it will take men of understanding and skill to accommodate them."

I paused for a few seconds before asking the critical question, "Do you want to join in or go home?"

Taylor Thornton spoke first, "Cole, I didn't come here for a picnic. You said the magic word—trouble. That's all I needed to hear. I'm with you."

Coop, Josh, and Jim were all ears. "About forty gunmen you say?" questioned Josh.

"Without further information, that's my estimate. There could be more or there might be less. Whatever the count, we'll take them on."

The three ex-Rangers exchanged nods among themselves. Cooper answered for the three, "We're with you, Cole. When do we leave?"

"Well, boys, I figured we'll leave just before daylight tomorrow. I want to cross the Rio Grande in darkness. No telling who or what is around to tattle on us. I want this visit to be a good surprise."

We all agreed on the departure time before the others went to their rooms to rest up. I decided to take in the town a bit before I hit the bunk. I walked through the roughest part of town—the area at the crossing. I felt that Juan might have stopped there before crossing the Rio and I wanted as much information as I could get.

I entered a lively cantina and immediately stepped to the right a few moments to let my eyes get accustomed to the dimness. A moment later, I took in the entire room at a glance. One Mexican hombre seated at a back table looked up at me from his card game. His eyes widened and his face turned white as a sheet. I'd seen that face before, in my earlier years. From the expression on his face, he remembered me as well. I started toward him.

* * *

Jose Gallinda looked across the room and stared straight into the eyes of Cole Stockton. The man was older now, but the look of death on his face was even more prevalent than in years past. Jose closed his eyes as he recalled the incident of a decade ago. A young Cole Stockton had made it clear to the Mexican that if he ever found him on the United States side of the Rio Grande again, he would kill him on sight.

Jose cringed at the thought. He began to tremble, fearing for his miserable life. Cole Stockton continued to walk straight toward him.

The other men at the table noticed the dreadful look on Jose's face, then turned as one to watch the Americano approach their table. The men exchanged glances. They looked closely at the American, reading the look in his eyes. One fellow made the sign of the cross before the trio edged away from their friend. They were sure that Jose would soon meet his maker.

I took advantage of an empty chair with its back against the wall out of habit. Most gun savvy men of reputation did likewise. Sitting across from Jose, I searched his face a long moment before speaking. Fear gripped Jose Gallinda.

I spoke first. "Jose, I need information. I want to know about a certain rancho about one hundred miles south of here. I want to know about the silver mine operations there. How many men work there? Who are the men that ride for Enrique de Marza? Get this information for me within the hour and I will forget that I saw you here in El Paso. Do we have a deal?"

Gallinda relaxed a bit. "Si, Amigo. I know of this rancho. I know of the silver mine. I also know some of the Ranchero's riders. I'll tell you all I know."

For the next half hour, Jose relayed all of his knowledge of de Marza and his men to me. I nodded, and then responded, "You may rest easy Jose. I will not take action with you here in El Paso. If your information proves correct, you can forget my vow of many years ago."

Abruptly, a flourish of riders arrived in front of the cantina. Jose looked to the door and saw the men enter. He once again shook with fear.

The arrogant young leader of the group made a sweeping survey of the patrons in the cantina, and when his gaze settled on Gallinda, he stared with hate. Before I made a move, the fellow walked toward us and announced, "Gallinda! I told you that you would be dead by sundown if I ever saw your face in Texas again. Stand up or die where you sit."

Jose immediately raised his empty hands before his foot pushed his chair back. I grabbed his forearm, preventing Jose from rising. I motioned for him to keep his seat. Once again, Jose became nervous and unsure of himself. I motioned for him to stay seated as I stood to face the young man who threatened my companion.

The stranger wore two Colt revolvers of the .44 caliber tied down to his body. He was young, but he wore his guns like he knew how to use them. I directed my remarks to the kid. "Jose here is my friend. I would appreciate it if you didn't kill him tonight. I might get mad and have to shoot you."

The kid laughed loudly, "Perhaps, you don't know who I am, stranger."

The others in the cantina rose quickly from their chairs to move away from the three of us. I figured that they expected gunfire at any moment.

"I don't care who you are," I retorted, matter of factly.

The kid glared at me. His eyes were bold and calculating. "I'm Johnny McCade. You may have heard of me by another name. Sometimes, I'm called the Durango Kid."

Well, I'd heard of him. Word through the grapevine had it that he was fast and sure. I could not recall any wanted posters on him which led me to believe that he was not of the outlaw brand. I figured him more for a young hellion looking for his brand of fun. That he led a group of like minded young men further encouraged that thought. I steadfastly held my gaze to his, and told him straight out, "You touch your guns, I'll kill you."

His eyes took me in, especially at the manner in which my Colt was belted around my waist. He spoke, "Just who do you think *YOU* are, friend?"

Everyone in the cantina held their breath as I replied, "The name is Cole Stockton. Now, do we drag iron, or would you like to have a beer and talk a bit?"

The rush of his breath was audible as he exhaled, then moved his hands away from his guns. His mood completely changed in that instant. He smiled for the first time as he took a chair across the table from me. His friends relaxed and turned to the bar for a round of beer.

After a bit of small talk, I told Johnny McCade about my quest south of the border. He seemed quite interested. Jose Gallinda again advised and answered questions about the rancho and silver mine activities.

Of particular note, Gallinda warned me about one of the ranchero's men, "Ricardo is one bad hombre. He is the ranchero's best pistolero, and he is without mercy. Many have fallen before his gun. Mi Amigo, Stockton, you would do well to avoid him."

Johnny McCade frowned seriously. "I have some friends that rode that way and never returned. I'll bet that some of them are in that silver mine. I want to ride with you. Ten men are here in El Paso with me. I can vouch for them. I'll ask them to ride with us. When do we leave?"

I responded with, "We'll leave at daylight, Johnny."

McCade nodded. He then motioned to his men at the bar to join him at an empty table in the corner. He spoke to the young men surrounding him in a voice that only they could hear. Moments later, he returned to let me know that his entire outfit would join us.

There it was. I had somehow recruited a small army of interested men with gun savvy. This venture had turned into a party that the evil ranchero would not soon forget.

* * *

Five of us: Taylor Thornton, Justin Cooper, Jim Farley, Josh Slater, and myself moved silently inside the El Paso livery as we saddled up our mounts in the dim stable light. Daylight had not yet come to the eastern sky.

Leading out of the stables, I looked skyward. Low clouds drifted on warm air currents in the darkness. I wanted to cross the Rio Grande within the shadows of predawn.

Johnny McCade and I had agreed on a schedule of sorts in order to avoid curiosity from observers. An hour after we left the livery, McCade and half of his men would cross the river. The remainder of his band would cross into Juarez an hour after that.

All in all, we numbered fifteen men hell bent on a mission. We were headed toward the same place—the sleepy little Mexican town near the place that Jose Gallinda called El Rancho Muerte, The Ranch of Death.

My plan was straight forward. We would enter the village in several groups of two to three men, arriving at different intervals. Once in town, we would take care to not all go to the same cantina. We would ask questions, the kind of questions that would cause the Ranchero de Marza to send rough men into town to check us out.

I figured to trim the edges off the forty gunmen before we made our primary move, namely to quickly capture the Rancho in the middle of the night. We would take the Ranchero himself hostage.

Call it a bold move if you will, but I was of no mind to pussyfoot around with the likes of this bunch. My plan constituted a direct demand situation. We would get what we came for, or I would lay waste to a great many of his men and a great deal of his holdings.

The men with me, no strangers to danger, were fighting men who faced adversity with determination and gun savvy. I had no doubt that we would prevail.

Chapter Nineteen

The Wrath of Salvation

Just after siesta, three days later, Taylor Thornton and I entered the village that Juan Socorro called home. We tied up in front of the first cantina we saw on the dusty main street. Five horses already stood at the hitching post. I saw right away that four of them carried the same brand.

I figured that the riders in the cantina were of the de Marza rancho. Taylor and I approached the saloon with the same thought in mind. We would have a cool beer, take a table toward the back of the room, and wait for an opportune moment to make our first move. Within the hour, at least ten men of our party would join us in town. That number would be enough to start the ball.

Upon entering the cantina, Taylor stepped immediately to the left, and I to the right. When our eyes grew accustomed to the shadows, we did a quick sweep of the room. One man stood drinking tequila at the bar. Four vaqueros sat at a table towards the middle of the room with mugs of beer.

The man at the bar looked every bit like a hired gun. His weapon was low to wrist level, his hand never too far from the butt of his revolver. When our eyes met, I figured this man for one mean hombre. He looked us over good. I suppose two gringos did stand out.

My eyes never left him. This gunman's body immediately spoke the language of irritation. He seemed very agitated at our presence. He didn't like strangers, especially Anglo strangers.

Our gaze locked together as one while he pondered me. I felt the icy chill of his soul. I knew that if anything happened, it would come from this man. He would be my first target.

Taylor and I walked to the bar and hailed the short, heavy-set bartender. He seemed a bit reluctant to approach us. "Dos cervezas, two beers," I called out. He contemplated the two of us for a moment, shrugged, then turned to produce two mugs. The barkeep squinted as he filled each with the frothy golden liquid from a large keg, then placed them in front of us. Taylor dropped a twenty dollar gold piece on the bar.

I carefully watched the gunman out of the corner of my eyes as I took the beer in my left hand. Momentarily, he turned to face us and he didn't look happy.

"Amigo!" I called out as I faced him, lifting my beer in a toast to him.

With an agitated expression on his face, he announced, "I am not *your* Amigo. I don't like you at all. I hate Yankees. I think that I must kill you today. What name should I put on your stone?"

I set the beer down on the bar and retorted, "Que es su nombre, what is YOUR name—Amigo?"

He laughed nervously. "I am Ricardo Alvarez. I am quite well known here."

I watched his face closely as I replied, "I am Cole Stockton and I think that you are letting your reputation overload your mouth—Amigo!"

Ricardo grinned before his face made that unmistakable ever so slight twitch. I knew then, what was coming. Suddenly, his hand swept to the butt of his revolver. The four vaqueros at the table rose quickly. Chairs flew everywhere. Hands went for pistols.

Taylor Thornton's right hand moved like a striking rattlesnake. His Colt flashed out as he stepped to the right. His left palm covered the hammer of his revolver as he leveled it. Fire, smoke, and hot lead spit from the deadly bore.

Thornton fanned the Colt five times amongst flying lead and sharp cracks. Bullets smacked into the bar behind him and into the mirror behind the bar. My friend kept unflinching attention to those gunman in front of him. One by one, the four vaqueros jerked with the impact of spinning lead.

Alvarez's revolver was rising out of the holster when his eyes widened in horror. My revolver was already leveled directly at him. I squeezed the trigger. The slug drove deep into his chest, as he lurched backward toward the wall of the cantina. I fired once more into Ricardo, then turned to the vaqueros, firing two quick bullets in their direction. I reckoned that I hit at least one of them.

Instinctly I turned toward the bartender to see him reaching for a shotgun under the bar. "I wouldn't do that, Amigo!"

The old man let it drop to the floor, raising his hands into the air as he backed toward the shattered mirror on the back of the bar. Glasses jiggled as he bumped against it.

Taylor Thornton approached the four downed vaqueros. Two showed signs of life. Taylor kicked all weapons out of the way and pulled one man to his feet. He set him down in a chair and with a smile announced, "I must be losing my touch, friend. Ten years ago, all four of you would have been dead. Just as well for you, though. I believe we have some questions to ask of you. We expect honest answers."

Just then, several shots cracked from somewhere down the street. That exchange was followed closely with another fullisade of sharp cracks from yet a third location further along the street. The ball had opened. Things were getting hot.

* * *

Justin Cooper, Josh Farley, and Jim Slater ambled into the *Mia Rosa*, a cantina across the street from where they observed that Taylor and I left our mounts. Locals recognized them as Texas Rangers. Five men drew pistols as they jumped from their chairs.

"Damned Comanchero traders!" shouted Farley. "Come and get it!"

Guns were out. The dank air of the cantina immediately filled with gunsmoke as hot lead whined around the room. Justin Cooper shot one man point blank then turned his gun to a second man, who suddenly buckled with Jim Slater's bullet first, then again with Coop's second bullet. Josh had both of his revolvers out, alternately firing into two other men. Slater turned his attention to the fifth man and summarily shot him three times as fast as he could thumb back the hammer and squeeze off.

Coop covered the bartender, who threw his hands into the air without contesting the old lawman's authority. He wanted no part of these Rangers.

* * *

Johnny McCade and three of his men walked into *Los Hombres* and lined up along the bar. Conversation among a group of vaqueros in this place stopped as they looked up to see the four Yankees at the bar staring at them.

Everyone in the cantina had heard gunfire from down the street. McCade and his men knew that they were about to have some action. More gunfire cracked from across the street. The vaqueros jumped up, scattering around the room. One man dived through a window and out of sight. Others backed against the wall as they drew weapons. Two men turned over tables as shields. Playing cards, and glasses of beer and tequila spilled over the floor of the cantina.

McCade and his men wasted no time. At the first movement, each reached for his Colt. Thunder rolled throughout the cantina just as it had in the neighboring saloons. Gunsmoke hung thick in the air as steady sharp cracks resounded one after the other.

Hot lead smacked into walls, bar, and men. One of McCade's men took a bullet through his thigh, cursed the man who did it, and instantly shot the man dead.

Within ten minutes, the village stood silent once again. Cole and his friends met Johnny McCade and his men in the street as more riders entered town.

Smiley Burnes looked down from his horse and cursed, "Doggone it! I sure wish that I had gotten one of the short straws. You guys are going to kill all forty of them before we even get to shoot. That just ain't fair."

McCade laughed and replied, "Don't worry, Smiley. There's enough to go around. We just trimmed off the edges a mite. There's plenty more where these guys came from and you can have first crack at the next bunch."

"Well, now," grinned Smiley, "that do make me feel a bit better. What do we do now?"

Cole spoke up, "Now we wait. We wait until dark, and then we go to pay a visit to the Ranchero—at his home."

In the late afternoon men were herded like animals from the silver mine to dingy prison cells. Rifle butts, cattle whips of ruthless guards punished those whose exhaustion caused them to stumble and fall. Prisoners prayed for their lives, May God have mercy on my soul and give each man with me the strength to reach his cell."

The grim recollection of comrades past who met their maker with gunshot when they faltered spurred the doomed men toward their cells each evening.

Manuel Vargas stumbled. A done-in Juan Socorro grasped the shoulders of the old man to prevent his fall and meeting the rifle butt of a malicious guard. Juan recalled the rowdy amusement of these henchmen when one among them used a whip on him when he fell. The young man whispered hoarsely, "Come, Manuel, get up! Don't let them beat you again. We can rest in our cell. Someday, we will be out of here. I can feel it. My blood has surged since early yesterday."

The prisoners of de Marza stood in line for their meager evening meal when a wild-eyed rider galloped into the mining stockade. He pulled his horse savagely to a halt, jumped off and ran to the foreman with gestures and exclamations.

Juan Socorro listened intently as the rider excitedly told of sudden gunfights in the village. It seemed as though several of the ranchero's men had been gunned down by Americans with lightning draws and steadfast nerve.

"What of Ricardo?" asked the foreman. "Why didn't Ricardo jump into this action and kill some of these Yankee men?"

The rider related with excitement, "Ricardo is dead. The cantina owner spoke of the gunfight. Ricardo was the first one killed. He challenged this Yankee when he reached for his gun. The Yankee was faster than a bolt of lightning and shot Ricardo twice. Ricardo never fired a shot. He died on the cantina floor."

A surge of hope ran through Juan. Ricardo was killed by an American so fast, that he shot him twice. Ricardo had not fired a shot. For Juan, that could only mean Cole Stockton was in his village.

Juan whispered to Manuel as he helped him into the cell, "My friend—the time of freedom is close at hand. My friends are here. They are in the village. Now, Raul will feel the hand of swift and deadly justice. The *Angel of Death* will descend upon him. May God have mercy on his soul."

Enrique Delgado Garcia de Marza, the elder Ranchero, was furious. The old man paced the hacienda as he mulled over the message brought to him. Who were these Americans who rode so boldly into his town and quickly shot down seventeen of his men in one deadly swoop?

The elder Ranchero shouted his rage to Raul. "These gringos will pay for this outrage with their very lives. This is my territory. This is my town. I will take all the men into town in the morning and put an end to these Yankees. Those not killed will be chained in the silver mine to toil their lives away until death takes them."

Emilita Vargas could not help overhearing the elder de Marza's loud ranting. She wondered, was this news the spark of hope that she prayed for? There were gunfights in the village. Had the friends of Juan arrived from the Colorado Territory? They had already taken a toll on the Ranchero's men. These Anglos were hard men, it seemed, to take on so many of the Ranchero's men and win. No one dared challenge de Marza's men in the past.

*　　*　　*

Two vaqueros rode with Raul when he decided to take a night ride out to the silver mine to inspect production. The three men trotted to the gates of the rancho, and spoke to the guards. The heavy wooden gates swung open and Raul and his men left the rancho. Turning west, they rode toward the hills.

Unknown to Raul, silent figures waited near the outer wall of the rancho. A rifle sight lined up on his chest. Were it not for a whisper, Raul would have seen the fiery gates of Hell at that very moment.

The moon slipped behind a dark cloud as midnight approached. The two men at the main gate of the de Marza hacienda stood smoking cigarillos and conversed in a whisper as they longed to complete this tour of guard duty. Presently there was a slight scrapping sound, a hushed brush of material on stone, and finally a thud. The guards stopped their light conversation to listen carefully.

One guard turned to the other, "I thought that I heard something." His compadre shrugged, "Forget it, Pepe. It is sure to be the wind. You know how it blows pebbles around the yard. It's nothing. You are too jumpy." They returned to small conversation and their smokes.

"Howdy boys!" The two guards had no time to respond before both were knocked unconscious by two quick blows to the head. Smiley Burns and his two sidekicks had crawled over the wall on either side of the guards and stepped up behind them with drawn revolvers. Smiley would have just shot them and be done with it, but he knew that Stockton was right. The noise would alert the rest of the hacienda. It wouldn't be a surprise anymore. Smiley loved surprises, especially when he was part of it.

Smiley and his side-kicks opened the heavy wooden gates. The remainder of the surprise party stepped into the rancho yard. Moving silently, they split up, some moving to the bunkhouse, others to the stables. Cole Stockton approached the main house, creeping without stirring a leaf on the bushes below the dark windows of the dwelling.

* * *

Emilita Vargas lay in her bed, eyes fixed to the ceiling. Without warning, she heard a slight noise. Slowly, the young woman turned to peer at the window. A shadow loomed against it. The shadow forced her window further open, and climbed into her room.

Emilia wanted to scream, but she had no voice. Her heart pounded so feverishly that she was sure that the intruder could hear it. Her muscles involuntarily caused the young woman to sit up as the intruder crawled into the room and moved toward her.

"S-h-h-h!" came the voice in a whisper. Briefly, the figure was illuminated by the moonlight allowing the frightened girl to glimpse into the face of an American. He smiled at her, "Are you Emilita?" She could only nod.

The shadow spoke again, "I am a friend of Juan. We received your letter and are here to help you. Please be very quiet. There will be more men coming into this room in a moment. You must dress in your robe.

Emilita's eyes were wide. She crossed her arms over her breasts. Here she was, alone with a man and more men coming, and she was in a nightgown. She rose and hurriedly pulled her dressing gown over her head.

Four more men eased through the window. Each glanced at Emilita and raised a finger to his lips forming the signal of silence.

Cole Stockton asked Emilita the layout of the hacienda. She gathered up pen and paper to quickly draw a map of the house, and explain who was in each room.

Suddenly, she remembered that a guard stood watch just outside her room. She urgently whispered the obstacle to Stockton. He nodded that he understood. Placing Josh Slater to the latch side of her door, he bid her to call for assistance from the guard.

Alfonzo Ortega never knew what hit him. One moment he was glaring with envy at the beautiful Emilita Vargas in her dressing gown, and in the next instant he lay sprawled on the floor, unconscious. Slater used the butt of his revolver to knock the guard out of commission. Within moments, Alfonzo was dragged into the room, gagged, hogtied, and thrust into a corner.

Stockton turned to his four companions to show them Emilita's diagram. Each man was assigned a target before they eased open the bedroom door to move silently into the hallway.

Emilita caught her breath and gave a long sigh. She thought, "The letter got through and Juan was right. He has many good friends." She turned to her wardrobe, and dressed hurriedly. At last, she would be free of this place.

* * *

The Ranchero, Enrique de Marza, slept soundly in his bed when the sudden click of metal sliding against metal resounded in his ear. His eyes popped open to find himself staring down the bore of a cocked revolver.

"Buenos Diaz, Senor Ranchero. I am Cole Stockton and I have come for my friend and some other things. You will do as I wish, or I will shoot you right here in your bed." The elder man understood.

"Good. Now, let's go downstairs. No, don't bother dressing."

They joined others from the hacienda in the large living room where Taylor Thornton had lighted the candles in a candelabra.

Josh Farley chuckled when he saw de Marza. "I never knew that rich men wore such frilly night shirts. You are a real dandy all right."

Emilita joined them presently, ready to travel. The elder de Marza looked at her questioningly. "You know these intruders?"

The young woman replied with spirited voice, "Yes. I know these men. They are friends of my true love, Juan Socorro. They are here at my request. I want my father and I want my beloved Juan returned to me."

The Ranchero spit at Emilita. "You are the intended bride of my son. You are a wicked woman. I shall see you die with your father and your friends."

Enraged, Emilita stepped forward and struck the elder across the face. As he recoiled from the blow, Emilita retorted, "You are the wicked one, you old fool. I would never agree to marry your evil son, Raul. I curse you for what you have done to my father and to Juan."

Cole Stockton intervened to ask Emilita, "Who is missing from this bunch?" She looked around the room and fear crossed her face once more. "Raul," she said with trembling voice. "Raul is missing. He is the worst of this lot. He is the one who beat Juan and my father and imprisoned them in the silver mine. He rode out earlier. I think that he was going to the mine. You must go there. If he finds that this hacienda has been taken, he will kill all of the prisoners. Juan and my father will be the first."

The Ranchero laughed out loud, "My son Raul will return with many riders and then, we will see who is in control here" He laughed only a moment as he glanced into the eyes of Cole Stockton. A long silence followed. The Ranchero laughed no more. That gaze at the lawman brought a vision of his soul burning in the fires of Hell. A shiver of death swelled in his body, causing him to pull back. The Ranchero knew then that Stockton could kill him in an instant. He never uttered another word.

* * *

I demanded Senor de Marza write a quick note to his son Raul. In effect, it stated that the hacienda had been captured. Raul was to release all prisoners from the mine and have them ready to exchange for the hacienda hostages at daybreak. I asked Emilita to read the letter, just to make sure that he had written what I requested.

I had Emilita select a messenger from amongst the household servants. She chose the ranchero's valet whom she was sure longed for his own freedom to carry the message to Raul. I figured that a personal servant to the man would carry more weight than a vaquero from the bunkhouse. Frightened beyond words, de Marza's valet mounted a horse and headed to the silver mine.

When the messenger was on his way, I turned to Taylor Thornton. "Taylor, I want you to take four of McCade's men and round up as many of the ranchero's cattle as you can find. Move them toward that silver mine, but keep them out of sight. I think that we might just need a cavalry charge and those cattle ought to do the trick."

Next, I turned to Coop and the Rangers, "Can you boys take a fast ride and get up in the rocks behind that mine? I want to take as many from behind as possible."

"Yeah, Cole," answered Coop, "We would love to have them boys lined up like sitting ducks. Anything happens and it will be a sure-nuff turkey shoot. Let's go, boys."

I turned to my new friend, "McCade, I want you with me. You and I are going to ride right down to the center of that mess and pluck off the chief rooster. I want him alive. Two of your men will ride with the hostages—keeping them in the shadows. The other four will split up, two coming in from the left, and two coming in from the right. I want to wheel this deal from a good cross fire."

McCade studied me for a minute. "Stockton, it don't sound to me like you are going to trade any hostages at all. In fact, it sounds a lot to me like you are going to go in there and when they show themselves, shoot hell out of them and take them people back when the smoke clears."

I nodded, "Well, Johnny, you've just about got it figured out. Taking our hostages is just for show. I've never made a deal for hostages in my life and I won't start now. Those are vicious men out there and by God, I am going to give them a taste of their own medicine."

McCade grew excited, "Let's do it! I'm itching to deal out some pay-back of my own, and there will be hell to pay."

Chapter Twenty

Justice Prevails

Raul de Marza raved like a mad man. How dare these Americans attack his hacienda, in the middle of the night like common thieves. He would trade for the hostages, but he would have a surprise waiting for these men.

He called his foreman to him and laid out plans to hide twenty of his men in the gullies on either side of the mine stockade. At the right time, as soon as his father was returned safely, he would give the signal, and twenty men would rise up with rifles to kill all Yankees and traded prisoners to the last man.

Raul cared not for the lives of the servants in the line of fire. Servants could be replaced. He would save trading that Juan Socorro and Manuel Vargas until the very last. He would kill them both personally before they reached the trade off line. He smiled with an evil grin. He planned to enjoy this.

* * *

The early gray of dawn found the hostage procession standing in clear view, two hundred yards from the silver mine stockade.

Cole Stockton and Johnny McCade sat on their mounts in front of the entourage. They chewed on tough beef jerky as their eyes judiciously scanned the mine sight. Both men knew their chances. Each had experience facing overwhelming odds. They would stand their ground.

The gates to the mine stockade opened and five men rode out with Raul in the lead. He stopped his men fifty yards from the gate and sat their horses. Momentarily, a large group of raggedly clad, ghostly looking men were herded out of the gate and lined up outside the wall of the stockade.

Stockton wondered if Juan and Manuel Vargas were among them. It occurred to him that if he were Raul, those two men would be in the very last bunch for trade.

"All right, Johnny. Let's ride down to them and get this thing going." The two men heeled their mounts into a slow walk and they studied their adversaries as they rode. Thoughts flashed through their minds.

Cole Stockton thought of Laura. He could almost feel the penetrating gaze of her crystal blue eyes looking deep into his. Her warmth flushed through him. He smiled and shifted his holster slightly.

They stopped at about ten yards from Raul and his four men. Both parties sat their animals looking at each other, not yet speaking. Raul glared at Cole Stockton. Raul was known for vicious savagery His stare had always unnerved those he faced. Now, it was Raul's turn to feel the penetrating power of instant death looking deep into his wicked soul.

Raul grew uneasy. This exchange was not going as he had planned. He had intended to unnerve these men and demand his terms of exchange. Without warning, a realization came to Raul. The only exchange would be a deadly exchange. He and his men were dead men, unless they could take these two Americano immediately.

Raul glanced around at his compadres. The strained look on his face told them that they must draw their weapons and kill the Americanos immediately.

Stockton and McCade saw the glances that passed between Raul and his men. There it was: the slight twitch of the lip, a nervous eye flutter, a sudden jerk of the hand. Raul and his men reached for their weapons simultaneously. That was all that Stockton and McCade needed.

Cole Stockton's hand flashed to his holster as McCade's hand flashed to his. Revolvers appeared in both of their hands. Deafening thunder roared as flame and hot lead spun back and forth. Horses reared and bucked as the lifeless bodies of their riders slipped from the saddle and fell hard to the ground.

Raul saw the flame from Stockton's Colt and in the next instant, the burning lead took him in the left side with such force that it slammed him out of the saddle to fall with a thud on the ground.

Johnny McCade proved deadly with his Colt as well. He quickly dispatched the two men on his side. He suffered a quick burn across his right shoulder, but kept firing. Both riders jerked off their mounts to lay in twisted heaps on the ground.

Stockton immediately blasted the man beside Raul, then quickly turned to the third man on his side and shot him through the middle. The man slipped from his horse and trampled by other horses milling and bucking.

The elderly Ranchero observed the deadly scene. He saw his son, Raul, slam from his horse. He saw the five men shot down by only two Americans. He jumped up out of the wagon. As the old man ran toward his son, he cried out, "Raul! Raul! My son, Oh, my son. You are no longer with me."

Shorty Whitman lined his rifle on the old man and was about to squeeze off when someone knocked his rifle out of line. Smiley called out, "Naw, don't shoot the old man, let me take him."

Smiley jumped down from the wagon and raced after the old man. Catching up to him, Smiley pounced like a wild cougar. He landed on top, knocking the wind out of the old man. Finally he sat on the chest of the old man, cocked his revolver, and demanded, "Once more and I'll blow you to kingdom come or we can walk slowly back to the wagon."

The old Ranchero shed tears as he shuffled back to the wagon, every so often turning to look back toward the limp body of his son. Without warning, Raul moved. He turned over, struggling to get up.

Stockton saw him and was instantly off his horse, reaching Raul before the Mexican regained his senses. Stockton jerked Raul to his feet, then laid the barrel of his revolver along side of his temple. Raul fell as though he was hit with a pole axe. He lay, out cold.

More gunfire erupted around Stockton and McCade. Because he witnessed the quick destruction of Raul and his four riders, the foreman of the mine ordered his men to open fire. At that very same moment, McCade's four men who were hidden in the surrounding gullies opened fire at the twenty men and their foreman.

The prisoners lunged to the ground for protection. Bullets smacked into the stockade walls behind them. Guards inside the stockade jumped into the fray with return gunfire. Within moments, hot lead smacked, splintered, and drove deep into their backsides. The three Ranger friends, positioned behind and above the stockade guards, levered their Winchesters as fast as they could.

A thundering roar in the distance caused the ground to shake like earthquake tremors. Three hundred head of cattle driven by Taylor Thornton and his men boiled over the rise and headed directly for the gullies where Raul had placed his twenty men. Guards and vaqueros dropped their weapons and ran for the stockade walls.

The prisoners saw that the guards were unarmed now, allowing them to move in groups to overpower the hapless guards. Screams rose from the fray as the once vicious guards received a taste of their own medicine. The Prisoners of the mine descended on the guards with fists flying until they were beaten bloody and rendered unconscious. Victory yells swelled from the throats of the former inmates of the mine.

The cattle herd thundered down into the gullies and up over the embankments. Numerous steers slammed into the gates of the stockade and it splintered into a hanging mass of debris. Juan and Manuel found themselves suddenly unguarded and alone to face the stream of cattle pouring into the yard.

Juan grabbed Manuel and together they ran as fast as they could out of path of the stampede, toward the gate. They made a dive to safety to the side of the procession. Rampaging wild-eyed steers streamed past them in a cloud of thick dust that choked both men. Juan and Manuel lay face down in the dirt, gasping for breath, but they were alive.

The three Rangers continued to pour deadly fire into guards and vaqueros who remained upright. Dead and wounded men lay scattered on the ground outside the stockade. Many had been trampled, and gored by the stampeding cattle herd.

Before long, a white cloth waved from within the walls of the stockade. The men of the Ranchero had no more heart for this fight.

Cole Stockton and Johnny McCade pulled Raul to his feet, threw him over his saddle, and then roped him face down. They delivered him to the stockade. The Rangers climbed down from the rocks above the mine, then organized the survivors.

Taylor Thornton and his group milled the cattle herd, slowing the stampede to a halt. McCade's men moved cautiously to the gullies to survey the damage. Several trampled bodies lay in death. The hostage procession moved slowly toward the stockade.

Cole Stockton and his small army of seasoned Westerners chained those guards and vaqueros who were alive. They cared for released prisoners, dressing their wounds as best they could. Juan Socorro helped Manuel to his feet and supported him as Stockton approached them.

"See, Manuel! Did I not tell you of my friends in the Colorado? This is my boss lady's very good amigo, Cole Stockton, an hombre most respected. He is feared by banditos who harm innocent people. He is also the law in the Colorado Territory. He sees that justice is done."

Cole grinned as he drew his Colt. "Don't look Juan. Cover your eyes." Stockton aimed at the shackles on Juan's ankles. When he fired, the shackles fell away. He did the same for the chains on the feet of Manuel. Then, Cole revealed to the two men, "There is a young lady in the wagon just outside the stockade. She is anxious to see both of you. We'll speak more later, but first you must console your lady love. Then, we must finish the job you came down here for Juan. I believe that the Ranchero de Marza owes us more than just one stallion. In fact, I believe he owes us a lot of horses. You pick out about twenty-five good ones for Laura."

Justin Cooper approached Cole. "Hey, Cole, I found a store of blasting powder in the stockade. What say we put a damper on this prison operation?"

Cole nodded, "That sounds good to me, Coop. Blow up the prison cells, the barracks, and the stockade. We need to leave the mine intact. The workers may find themselves with an honest job after the Mexican authorities are apprised of the situation here."

Enrique and Raul de Marza were shackled together and placed with the surviving henchmen. Former prisoners who were prepared to testify against the outfit guarded the group. A rider was dispatched to summon Mexican authorities. Within three days, a troop of Mexican soldiers arrived to take them into custody. It would be heard later that the Mexican government subsequently confiscated all of the holdings of the de Marza family. Enrique and Raul would spend years in a Mexican prison for their crimes.

A few days later a most jubilant procession crossed the Rio Grande into the United States. Ranchero wagons transported Americans held prisoner back to the United States. Juan Socorro, Taylor Thornton, and some of Johnny McCade's men rode herd on twenty-five of the finest horses in all of Mexico. Emilita and her father drove a wagon filled with their belongings. The three Ranger friends rode with Cole Stockton and Johnny McCade. Each enjoyed the company of the others as they joked and shared tales on their journey to El Paso.

Back across the Rio Grande in El Paso, Texas, Cole Stockton and friends stood witness to a small wedding. Juan Socorro and Emilita Vargas were married with the blessings of her father, Manuel. The three would move to Colorado to begin a new life employed on the Sumner Horse Ranch.

Taylor Thornton returned to his wife on their ranch with new vigor and zest for life. Justin Cooper and his Ranger friends returned to Fort Stockton, Texas where they opened an office as range detectives. They came to develop a thriving business.

Johnny McCade and his group reunited with old friends and rode off in search of new adventures.

Cole Stockton rode with the Juan Socorro family. A sense of justice and satisfaction filled his soul. Continuously his mind held a single thought as they neared the Sumner Ranch, "I hope she's got some coffee on the stove, because if I know her and her boys, it's going to be a long night of reunion, introduction, and celebration for the ranch family."